Shhhhh.

They'll Hear You.
Bedbugs 1, 2, & 3.

By E.A. Green.

Published through Jack in The Green Publishing.

Copywrite © 2023.

All rights reserved. No part of this book may be reproduced, stored in a retrieval system, or transmitted in any form or by any means without the prior written permission of the publisher, except by the reviewer who may quote brief passages in a review to be printed in a Newspaper, Magazine, or Journal.

Every illustration within this storybook book came from the internet's free domain.

If any copyrighted material was accidently used, it was done unintentionally by this Author and Illustrator who is more than willing to remove them at the owners request.

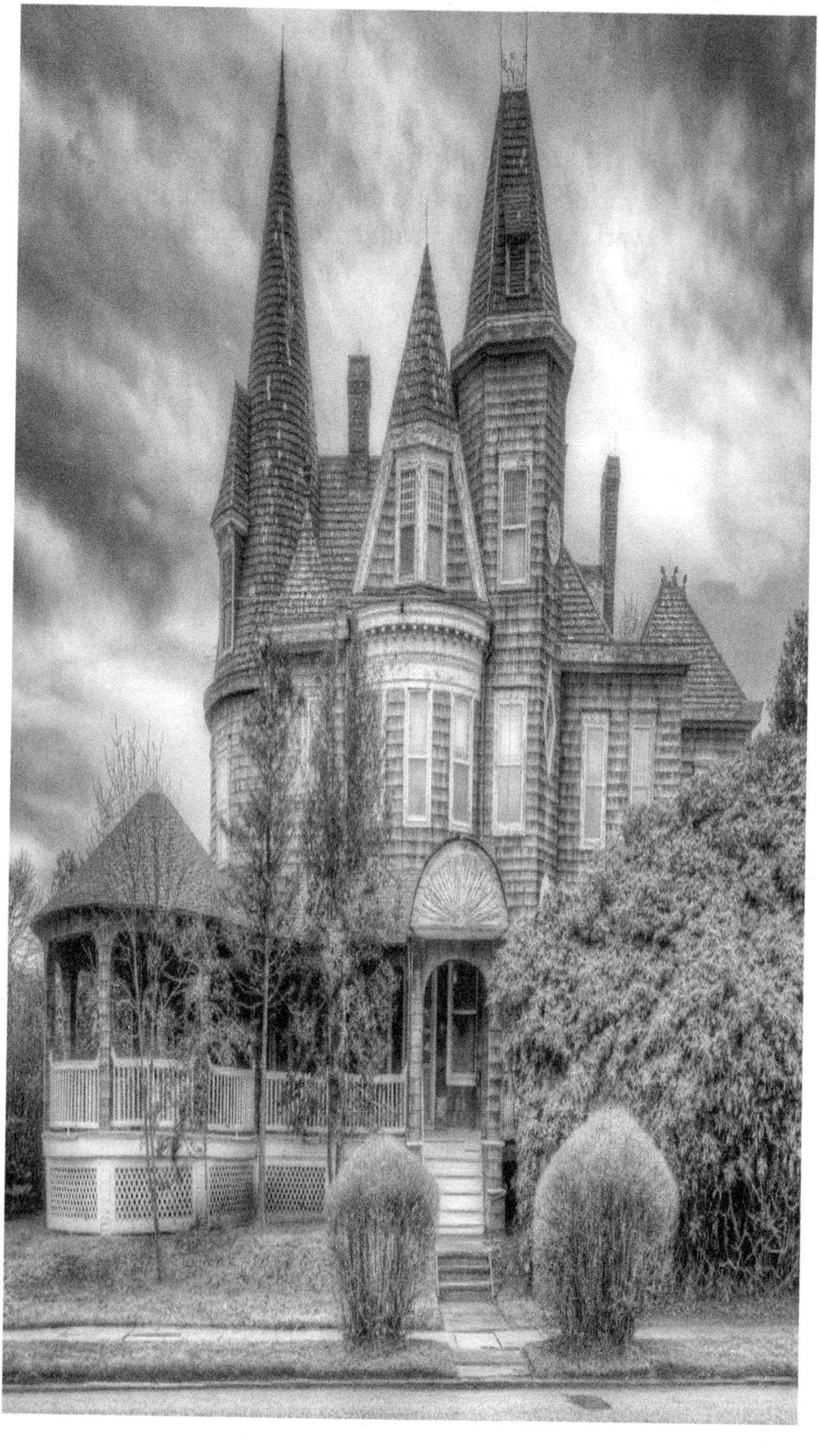

DEDICATION.

I and the spirits of Gomez and Morticia, dedicate this Bedtime Storybook To All of the Unnamed Wednesday's and Pugsley's In Us Wanna-Be Addams's.

6

The Greenman's Favorite Bedtime Fables, Fairy Tales, and Nightmares.

Don't Let the Bedbugs Bite

E.A. Green

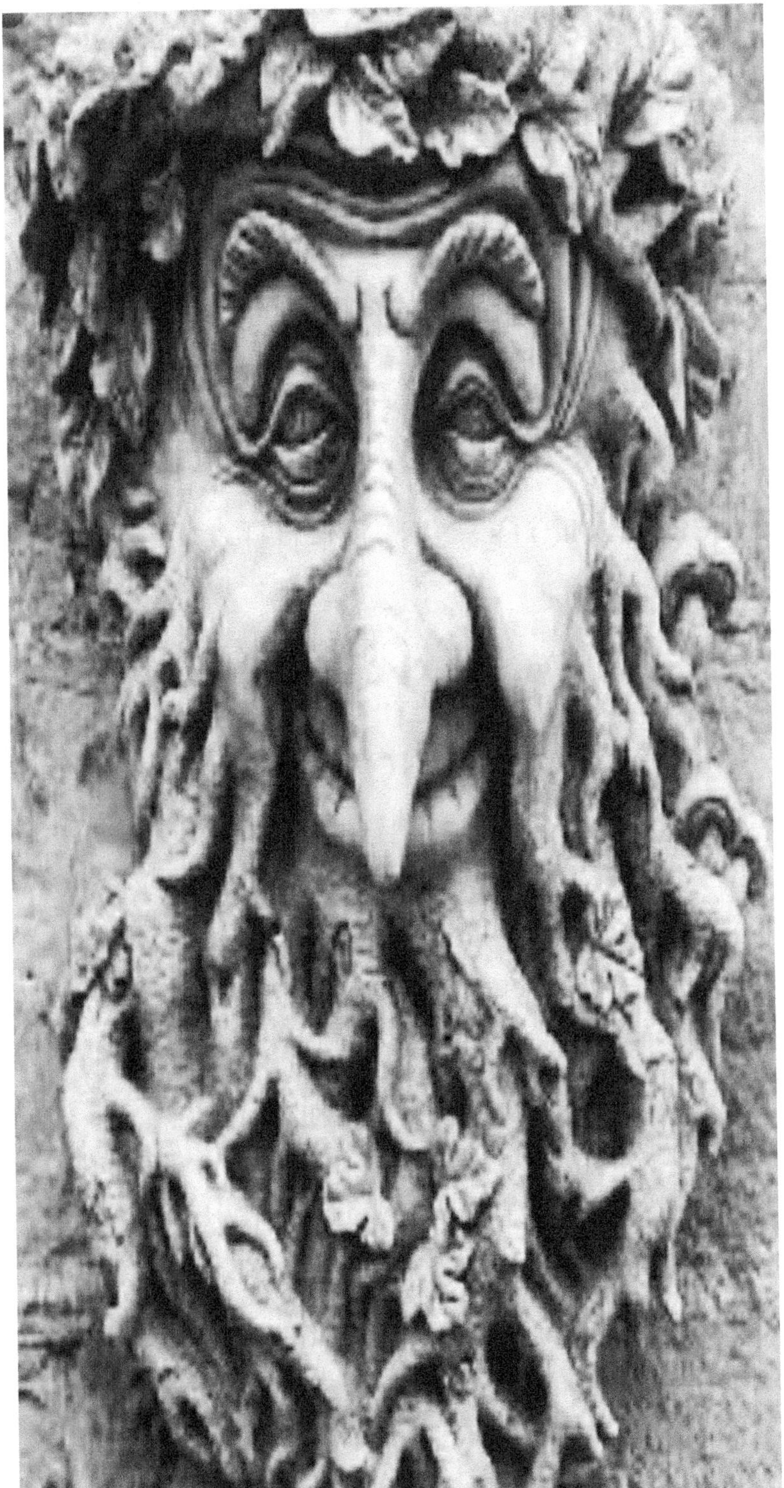

TABLE OF CONTENTS.

QUOTES FROM THE GREENMAN.

A FAIRIES TALE.

QUOTES FROM THE GREENMAN.

BLOODY MARY.

QUOTES FROM THE GREENMAN.

GORGE GEORGY.

QUOTES FROM THE GREENMAN.

MR. BLISTER.

QUOTES FROM THE GREENMAN.

HELLHOUND.

QUOTES FROM THE GREENMAN.

EDDIE BEAR.

QUOTES FROM THE GREENMAN.

MR. BOOGIE.

QUOTES FROM THE GREENMAN.

LITTLE LIZZY.

QUOTES FROM THE GREENMAN.

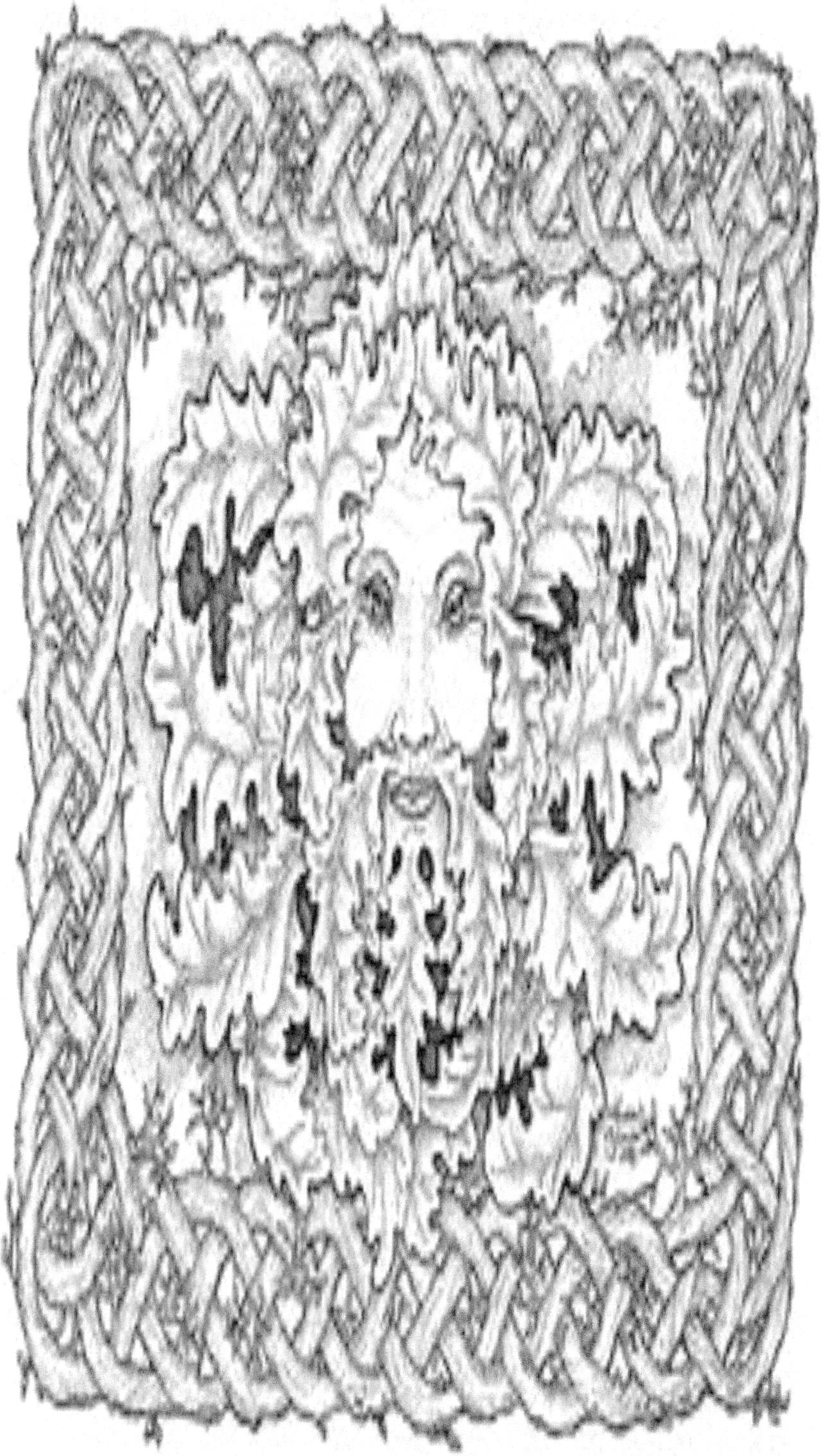

QUOTES FROM THE GREENMAN.

The future is not set in stone

Until we have taken that last breath

And close the book.

So,

Turn the page

And

Read On.

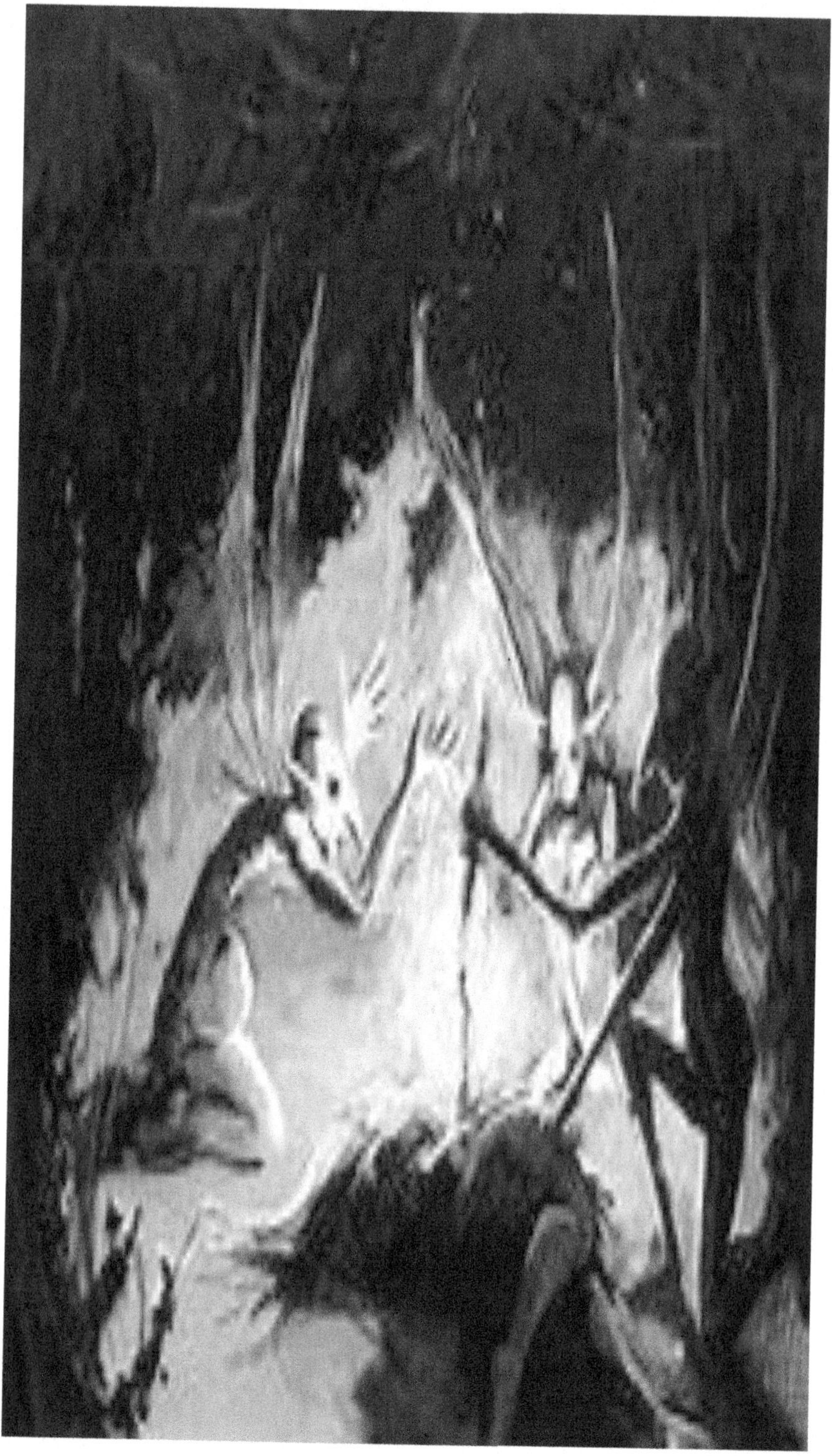

A FAIRIE'S TALE.

If the animals are whispering

As flowers do hush,

Voice not to speak

And turn from thus.

If forest gleam

At pitch black hour,

Sparkling and twinkling

Despite night's power.

And in the sun

Blind you be,

Drawing the strength

of will from thee.

Touch not!

Go not!

Turn away!

The Fairies are never

There to play.

You see my friend

Their trap is set.

So mind your greed

And take not step.

For when they appear

And you are caught.

Your spirit will leave

This forest not.

And as a rule of Fairy Law,

A tree you'll be

For one and all.

So when you see

And your eyes do pleasure.

Remember.

It's your soul Fairies

Deem as treasure.

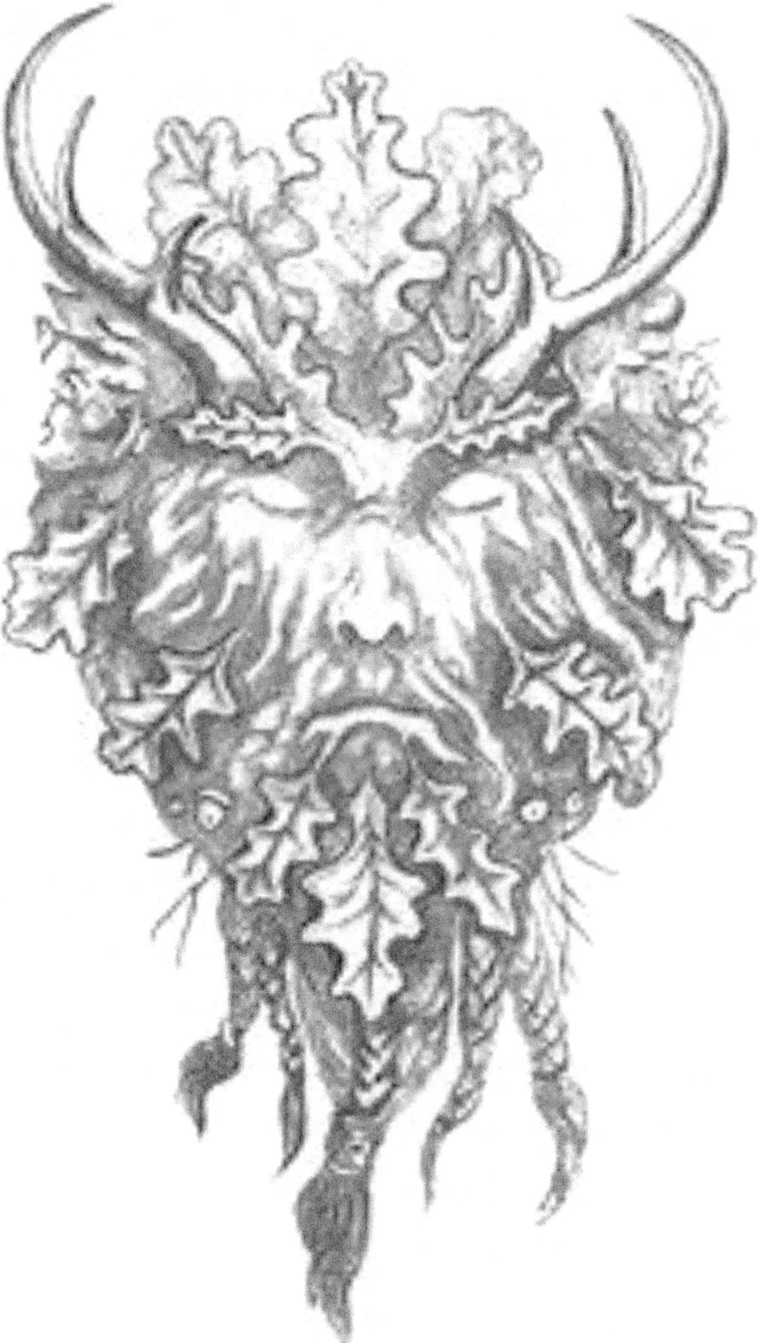

QUOTES FROM THE GREENMAN.

Life is but the wind on an ever-changing surface.

A passing shadow in the structure of time.

Only to be remembered as Fables or Legends

To future generations

Which will only come to be recalled as dreams.

I wonder how they will remember you.

20

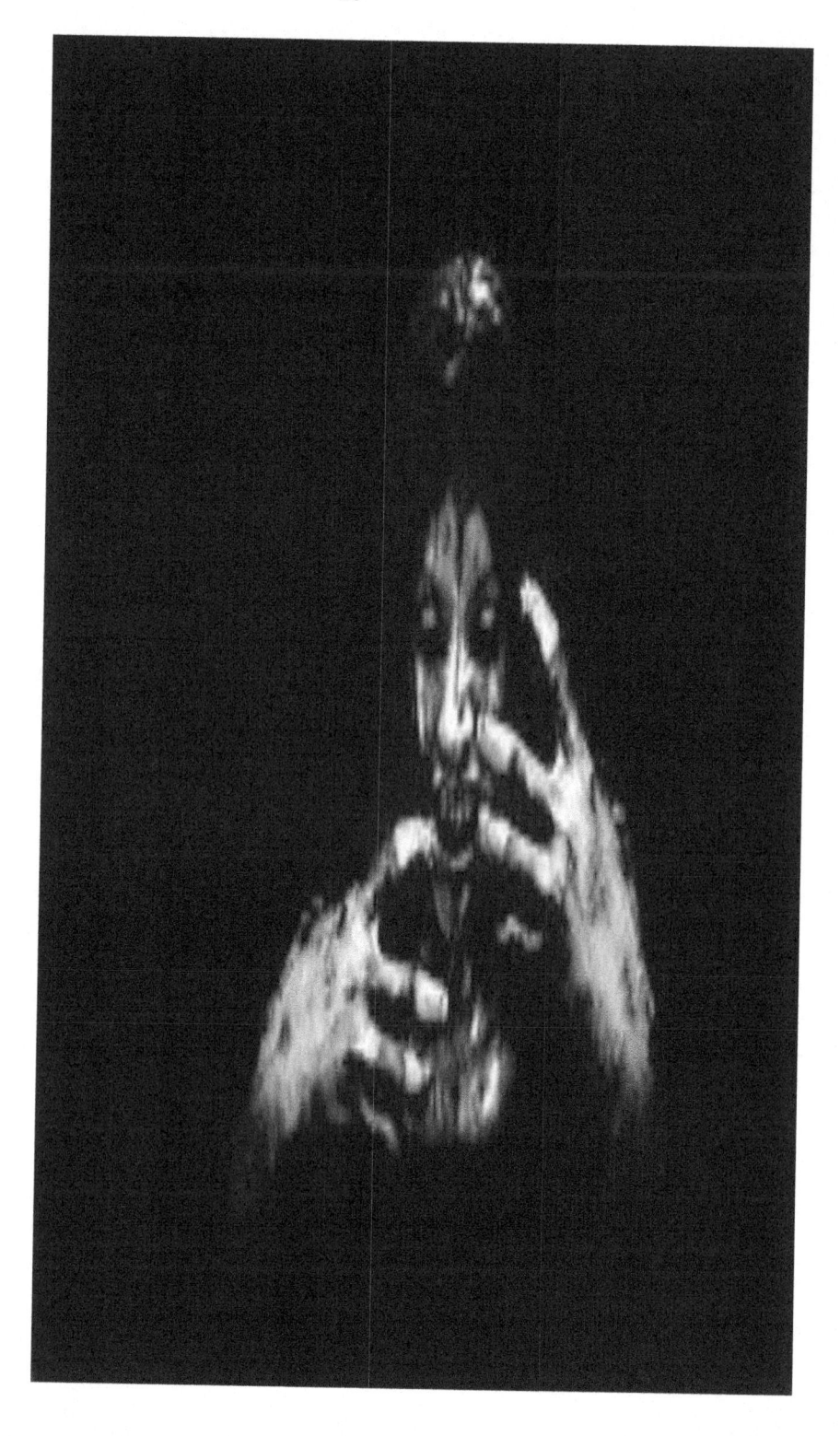

BLOODY MARY.

If you want

To scare your friends

And have a freaky time.

Go into

A darkened room

And say this creepy rhyme.

Here I stand

Between two mirrors

A candle will I light.

When I see

Her bloody face

I'll smash my head

Into that place.

All these things

Will you do

After you've rhymed this

Three times through.

Bloody Mary.

Bloody Mary.

Lite the candle bright.

Spin around.

Don't look down.

You'll miss a frightful site.

Bloody Mary.

Bloody Mary.

The candle must still burn

Spin around.

Don't Look Down.

It's just your second turn.

Bloody Mary.

Bloody Mary.

Dim the candle low

Spin around.

Don't Look Down.

She's about to show.

Bloody Mary.

Bloody Mary.

Now that you've done three

Spin around.

Don't look down.

Onward we must be.

Now smash your head

Into the place

Where she reflects back

On your face.

Bloody Mary.

Bloody Mary.

Listen to her glee.

Spin around.

Don't look down.

Your bloody dead

Like she.

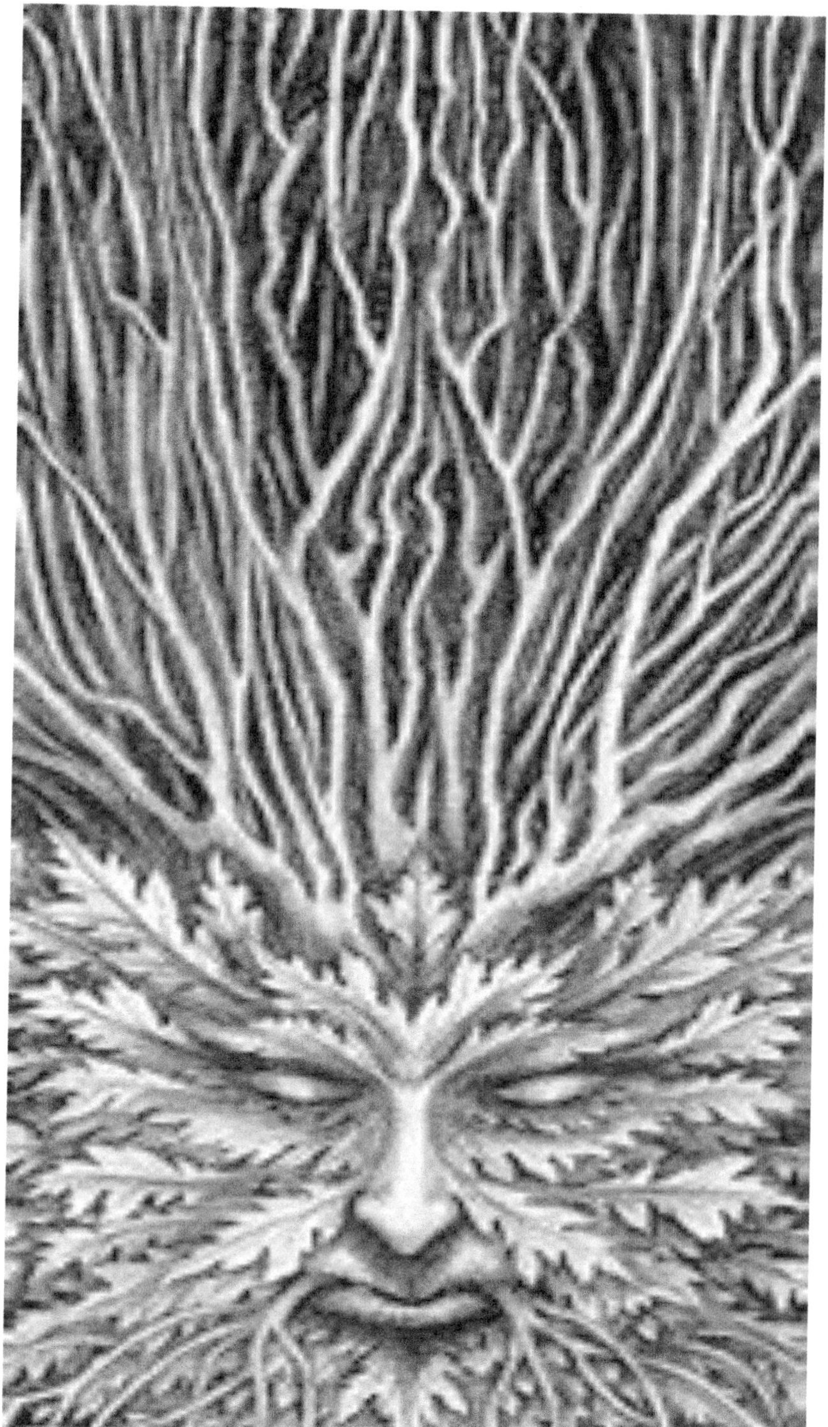

QUOTES FROM THE GREENMAN.

If you want to make an evil demon jiggle.

Pull his tale

Slap his horns

And give his chin a tickle.

I'm sure to bet

By the time your through

His fanged sharped lips will wiggle too.

28

GORGE GEORGY.

Mommy say's

It's beddy-bye time.

So, everyone sing

His deadly rhyme.

Now lay down

Your sleepy head.

So, Gorge Georgy

Thinks you're dead.

Cause if you don't

And he sees you peeping.

The hairy little critter

Will come along creepin.

So, cover your head

Or dinner you'll be.

He laughs out loud

HEE. HEE. HEE.

Gorge Georgy

Ribbons and bows.

He loves to chew

On sweet girls toes.

You will know

When he's around.

They'll be all wet

And slimy dark brown.

So, don't be scared

When Georgy's a nippin.

Or, he'll bite off your toes

While his tongue's a lickin.

So, cover your head

Or dinner you'll be.

He laughs out loud

HEE. HEE. HEE.

Now onward with

George's nursery rhyme.

He's deadly hungry

And you're tasting so fine.

Gorge Georgy

Dollies and tea.

For you he is coming

That's his giggling glee.

Your fingers are next

Maybe, you'll keep them.

Clicking sounds do scare him

Better start snappin.

And if you can

Send him away.

Switch rooms with your brother

Before that next day.

The eight-legged critter

Is coming back you see.

His hunger still burns

And he needs to feed.

So, cover your head

Or dinner you'll be.

He laughs out loud

HEE. HEE. HEE.

Gorge Georgy

Boys are toads.

The slimy tad poles

Have smelly green toes.

He's said to profess

That those are the best.

While dribble drooling

For a taste of grotesque.

So, wash your hands

And both your feet too.

Before getting in bed

Or, he'll eat on you.

The hairs on his legs

Will prick up and swell.

Saying supper is ready

They can tell by the smell.

So, cover your head

Or dinner you'll be.

He laughs out loud

HEE. HEE. HEE.

If his legs do skitter

Across the wood floor.

He's coming for You

From his home closet door.

So, if you value your life

And you'd like to keep tickin.

You better stay still

While Georgy's a lickin.

Because if you don't

And he starts to nibble.

Your fingers and toes

Will no longer tickle.

So, cover your head

Or dinner you'll be.

He laughs out loud

HEE. HEE. HEE.

Gorge Georgy

Chocolate and cream.

God how he loves

To make little kids scream.

I can still hear his laugh

I can still feel his fangs

I can still see his many eyes

Looking right into me.

So, check your toes

And fingers too.

When the sun does rise

After his nightly boo.

And if they're not there

And not loudly clicking.

Gorge Georgy

Was the one nippin.

For the night is his

The day time too.

If your digits are missin

Georgy spider found you.

So, cover your head

Or dinner you'll be.

He laughs out loud

HEE. HEE. HEE.

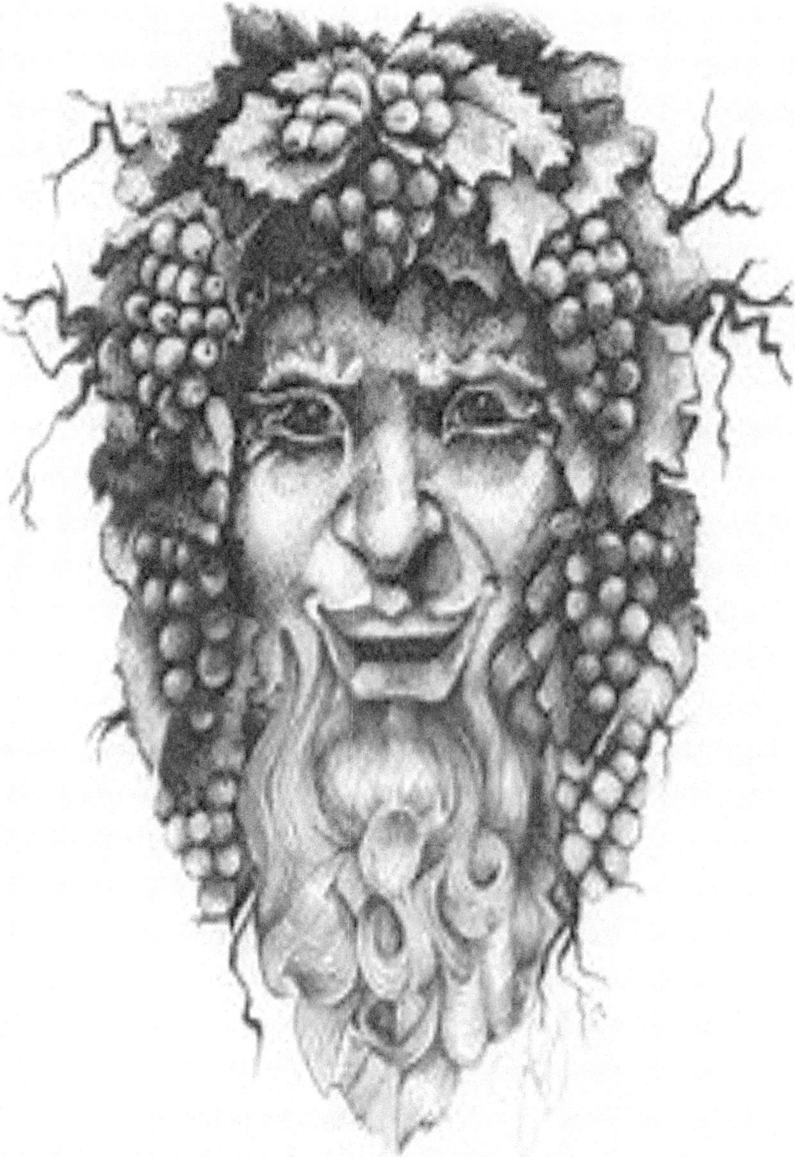

QUOTES FROM THE GREENMAN.

To make a sad clown happy,

You must first

Turn his frown upside down.

So, cut off his face,

Then spin it around.

Now you have

a smiley clown

Who's no longer sad

Who's no longer down.

40

MR. BLISTER.

When you wake up

And find there are sores

You now have a new friend

Who's much to abhor.

It's called a little bedbug

And it is here to stay

And they never will ever go away.

He's the little vampire

Who hides during the day

Just waiting for your sleepy head

To lay back down his way.

It waits until it's dark

When you're no longer waken

Then creeps under the sheets

A slurp of you it's drinking.

And if your slimy ooze

Reminds it of bacon

Every last drop it's thinking of taking.

He's the little vampire

Who hides during the day

Waiting for your sleepy head

To lay back down his way.

Mr. Blister is its name

And feeding on people

Is his nightly fame.

And he's chosen you

For his next dinner date

So, remember these rules

Or you'll be on his plate.

He's the little vampire

Who hides during the day

Waiting for your sleepy head

To lay back down his way.

You better look good

Before crawling under the covers

Checking those edges beyond all the others.

Because if you miss one

Or even just two

They are all going to feed

On every inch of you.

He's the little vampire

Who hides during the day

Waiting for your sleepy head

To lay back down his way.

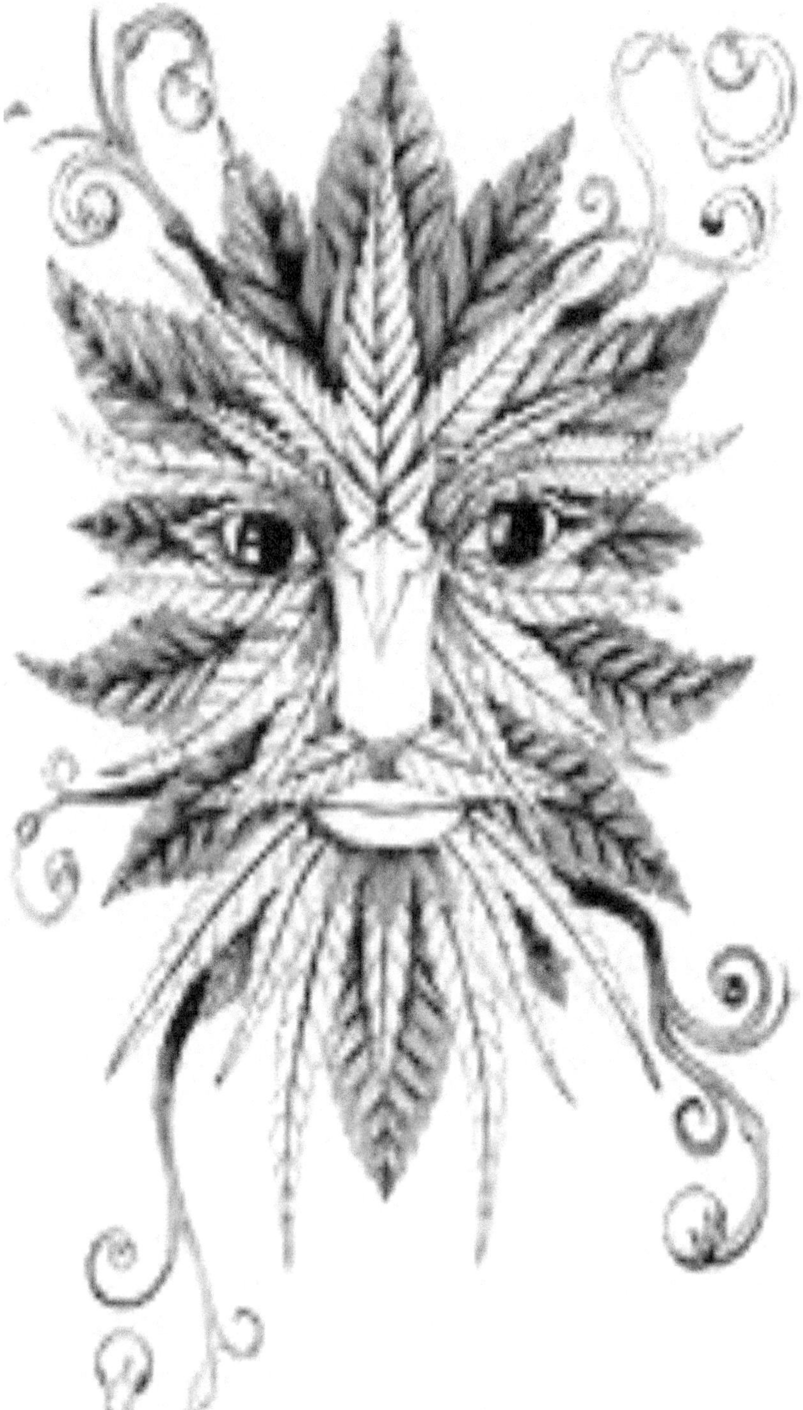

QUOTES FROM THE GREENMAN.

Kitchen Witchin is part of the baking process.

So, you better get out of Grandma's way

Or she'll chop you right up

Mix your meat in

And serve you as pie

To her tea party friends.

48

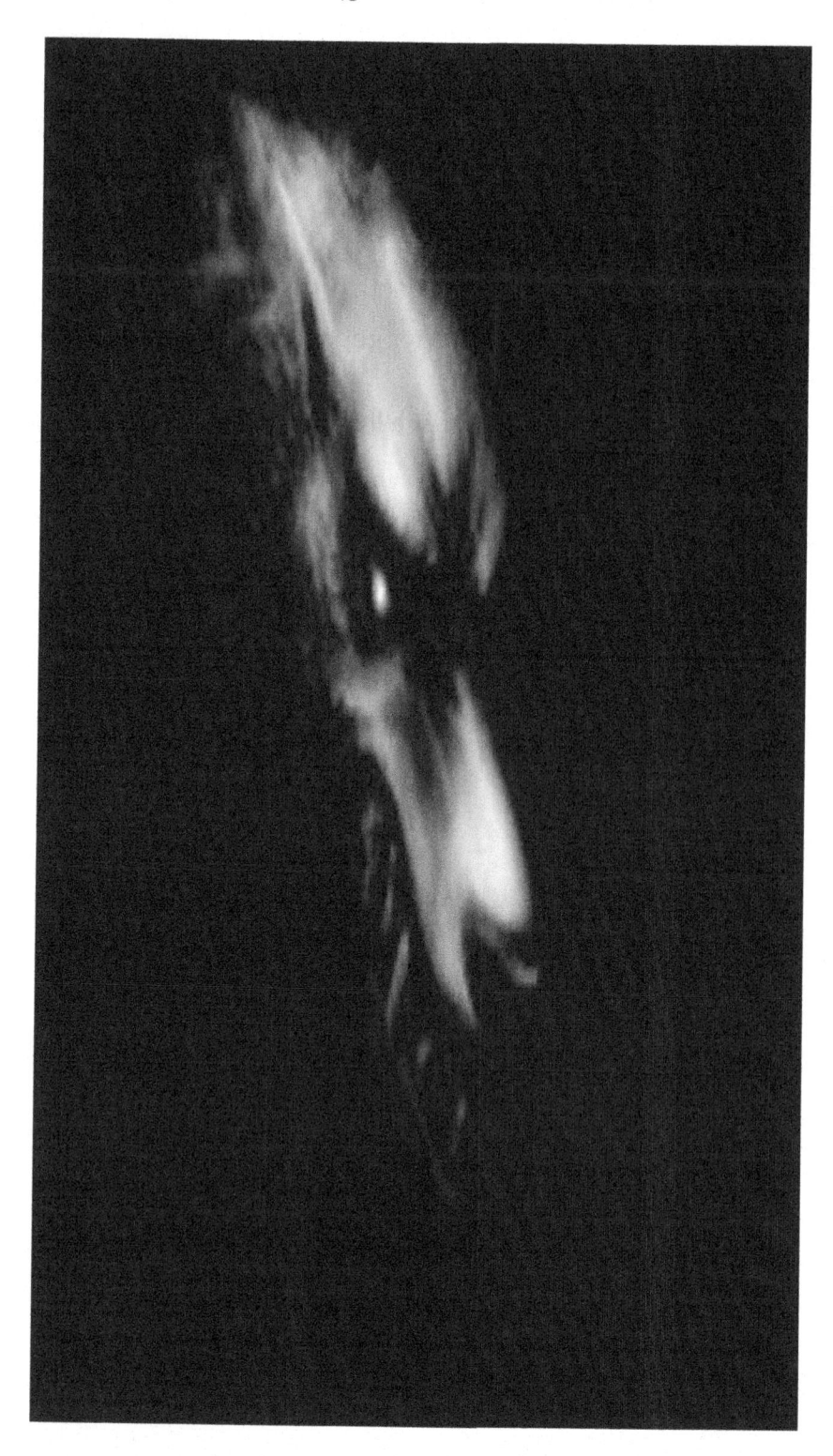

HELLHOUND.

If you are on

The out and go.

The night has fallen

His howls do blow.

You better run

And find a place.

Before he smells

Your scared fears face.

So, try not to cry

Or give yourself up.

Because, he most certainly

Will eat you for sup.

If the moon is full

Young and bright.

You'll certainly find

A Werewolf fright.

He's out on the prowl

Hunting for food.

Looking and sniffing

For fresh meat like You.

So, try not to cry

Or give yourself up.

Because, he most certainly

Will eat you for sup.

As he gets

To where you do hide.

His nose does a sniffle

Because your fear ripples.

So, what to no end

Are you gonna do

As his whiskers rub by

And tickles times two.

So, try not to cry

Or give yourself up.

Because, he most certainly,

Will eat you for sup.

The best advice

I give to a single.

Is don't go outside

When funny bone jingles.

Or, you'll end up fleeing

As tears do dribble.

Hoping you're not

His bloody next nibble.

So, try not to cry,

Or give yourself up.

Because, he most certainly

Will eat you for sup.

The hounds of hell

Most certainly will

Chew your bones

From their meat filled pate

The next time you

Stroll alone

On a quiet moonlit

Hellhound date.

So, try not to cry

Or give yourself up.

Because, he most certainly,

Will eat you for sup.

I didn't listen

To my own words

When the laughy bone

Rang and ringled.

Now I'm sliding

Down It's throat.

My dying screams

Dwindle.

So, try not to cry

Or give yourself up.

Because he most certainly

Will eat you for sup.

The next time his night

Does call out to you.

Remember these things

Long, Hard and Through.

The hairy big beast

Mr. Werewolf by name.

Will use your bones

To clean his plate.

So, try not to cry,

Or give yourself up.

Because, he most certainly

Will eat you for sup.

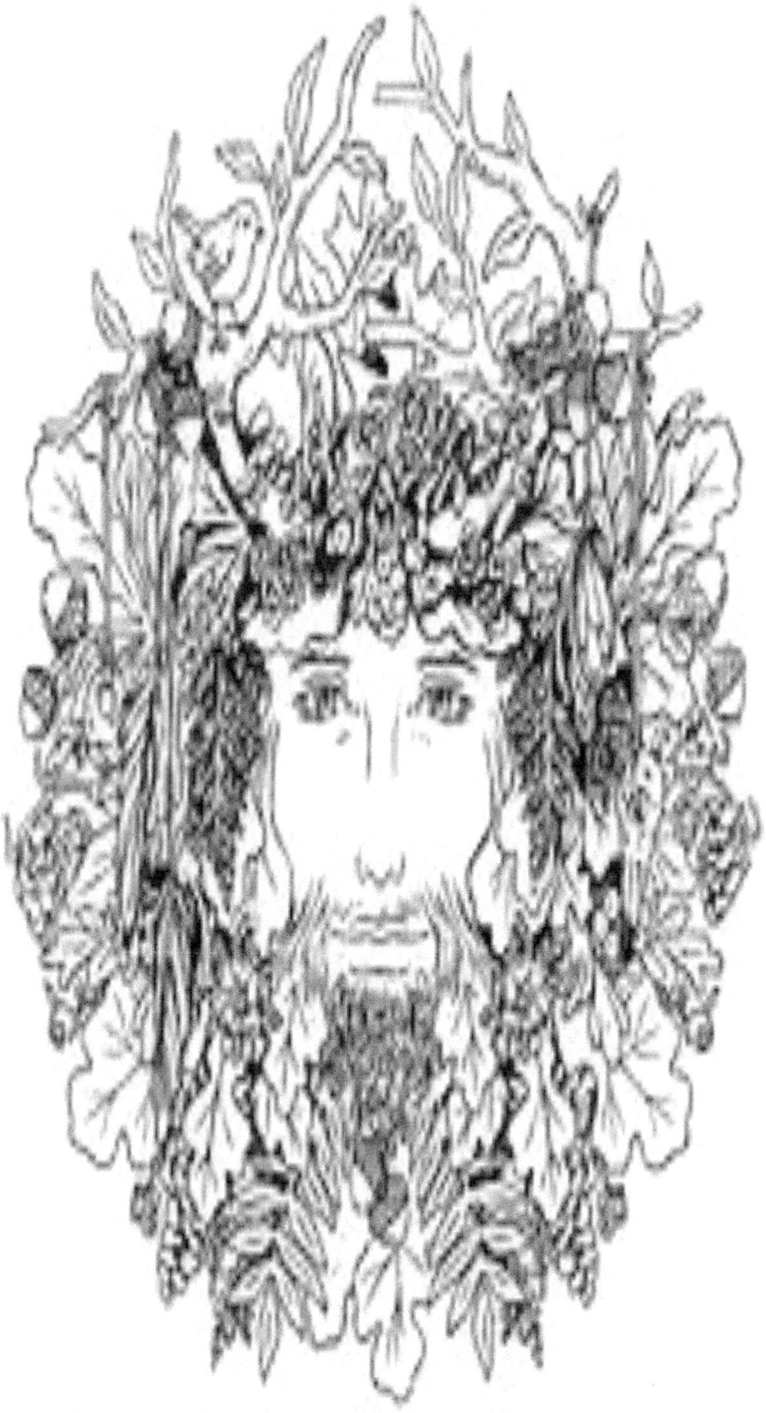

QUOTES FROM THE GREENMAN.

If the Boogeyman comes a knockin

And you don't ask him what for?

He'll kick down the door

And stroll right on in

So, always lock it before.

58

EDDIE BEAR.

Once upon a time, every child had an Eddie Bear to love, watch over, and protect them. They could always be seen running, playing, and chasing the children they so loved and adored.

Some of them even wore cloths and shoes like a real kid.

Eddie bears sat at the table, ate with their families and slept snuggle in the beds of every household member.

And that was because everyone had to have their own personal bear.

But, not every boy and girl cared for their Eddie bears.

Those Eddie Bears who just happened to be the unlucky ones, were beaten, starved, and abused by their protectors.

Many of them had been tortured and ripped apart by the hands of those that professed to care them. While some of the Eddie Bears had an ear or two missing; others had their eyes plucked out and an arm or leg ripped off.

There were even those that had been purposely disfigured by knives, scissors and fire.

Not everyone loved their Eddie bears like they should have.

And that's when it happened.

One day an Eddie Bear could no longer take the horrors that were being bestowed upon it, and Savagely Attacked the child that was dragging it through the mud before trying to drown it in the bathtub.

When word got out that, "once again," someone had tried to kill an Eddie bear; the other abused bears, "and those that were not," rose up and attacked their protectors, captors and killers.

The people were so shocked that such a docile creature could do such a thing; that a decree was sent out to the masses. Every last Eddie Bear must be hunted down, killed and destroyed.

Even their pelts must be burned.

There could be no trace, "what so ever," of their existence.

And so the people did.

Well, almost everyone.

A few of the doll makers decided to create an Eddie bear version and, "unbeknownst to everyone else," used their pelts for the coverings. And that's why, "as of today," some children pass away in their sleep.

They don't have a Teddy bear in their rooms.

They Have An Eddie Bear!

Because so many Teddy bears were made; the Eddie Bears quickly disappeared into the masses that were bought and purchased for baby's, children and even some adults.

No one, "other than their makers," had any idea that the possessed Eddie Bears were seeking revenge on those that had killed them and their kind. And that's because their creators where, "accidently," killed just days after bringing them, "Somehow?" back to life.

That's why You should always Treat Your Bear Right.

"You never know," your Teddy bear could actually be an Eddie bear.

So, if you're in bed and hear a noise in your bedroom; make sure that, "before going to sleep," you have a Teddy bear and not an Eddie bear. Because, "if you do," they will hunt down anyone who hurts, mistreats or maims them.

That's why You should Always Love and Respect Your Bear.

62

QUOTES FROM THE GREENMAN.

If a Monster comes a creepin

Grab your baseball bat and ball.

They've always got time

To stop and play

Before they eat you all.

64

MR. BOOGIE.

He's the little centipede

Who lives under your bed.

At night he likes to stay real warm

While sleeping in your head.

So, what can you do

To hold him at bay.

But keep those eye's opened

So he'll stay away.

But first he must crawl

Across the place where you sleep.

He's going for his snuggly bed

By starting at your feet.

So, what can you do

To hold him at bay.

But keep those eye's opened

So he'll stay away.

The jittery little bug

Who dances like the devil.

Has a thousand tapping legs

And loves to cause trouble.

So, what can you do

To hold him at bay.

But keep those eye's opened

So he'll stay away.

His pointy sharpened feet

As he goes up your leg.

Will cause you to scream real loud

While he happily comes your way.

So, what can you do

To hold him at bay.

But keep those eye's opened

So he'll stay away.

Mr. Boogie's on your back

Your neck is in his view.

Once he reaches that sweet, sweet spot

Your ear will feel him too.

So, what can you do

To hold him at bay.

But keep those eye's opened

So he'll stay away.

It's almost that time

To crawl into bed.

He just has to get

Through the hole in your head.

So, what can you do

To hold him at bay.

But keep those eye's opened

So he'll go away.

Now he's inside

Warm, safe, and gowned.

He's tucked into bed

And sleeping so sound.

So, what can you do

To hold him at bay.

But keep those eyes opened

So he'll go away.

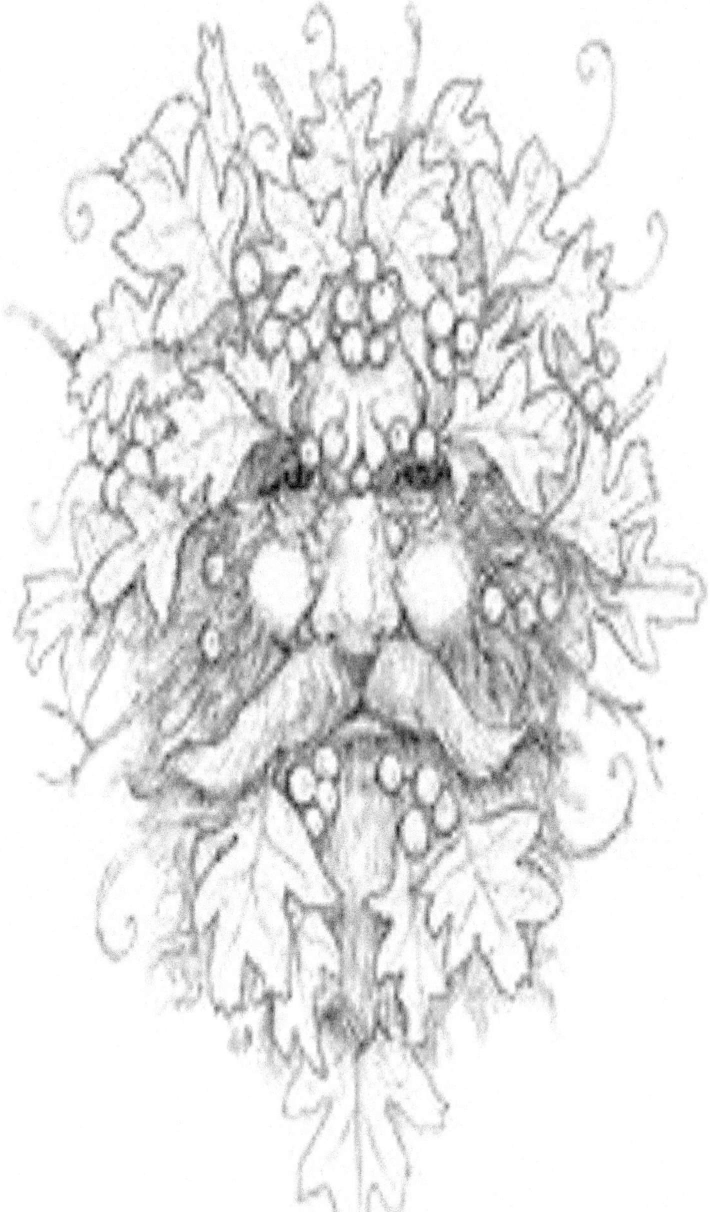

QUOTES FROM THE GREENMAN.

If a zombie ask you for a bite to eat,

You better give him a finger.

Oh, silly me.

Zombies never ask for just one bite,

They always ask for two.

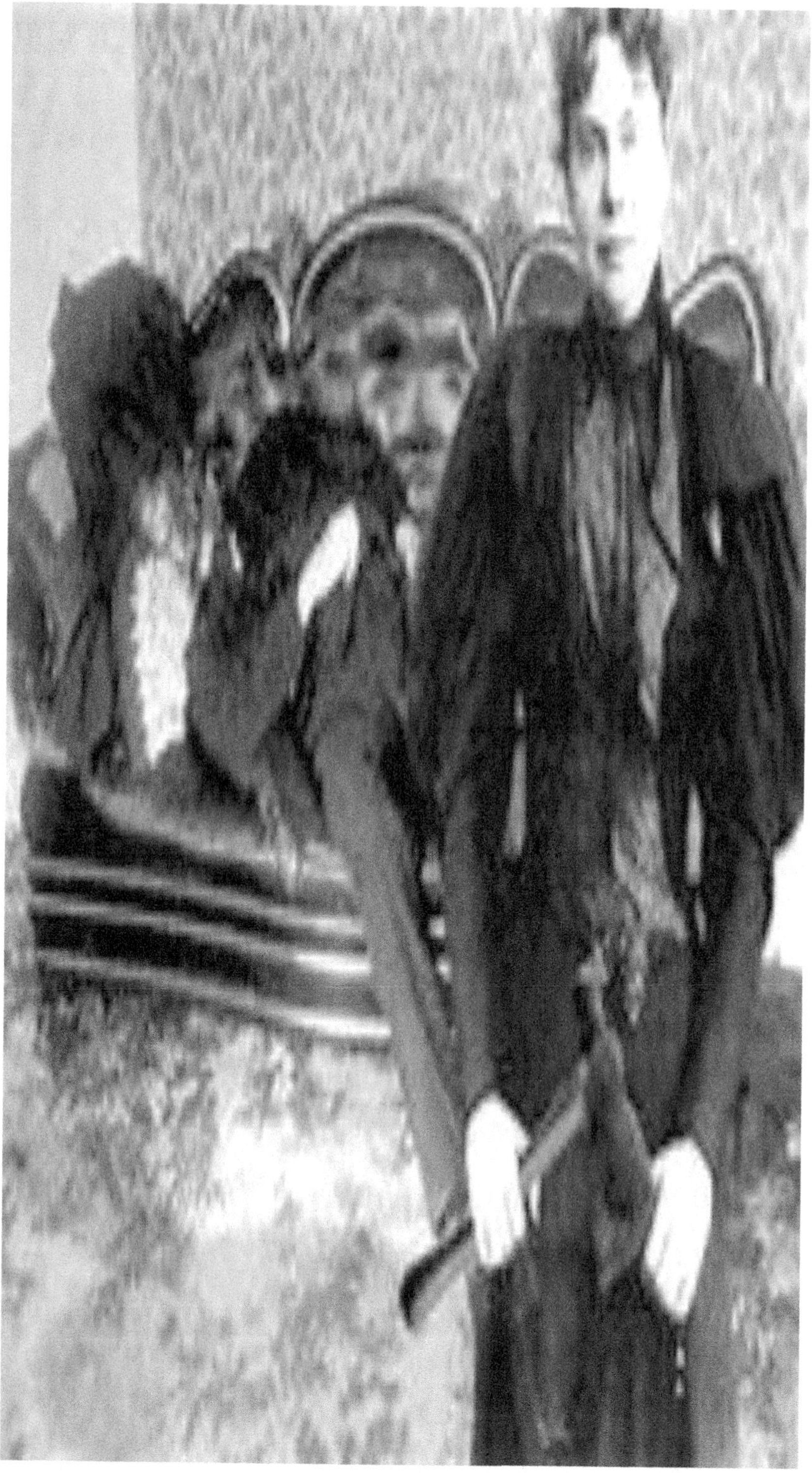

LITTLE LIZZY.

If Mommy wants to talk with her friends

And sends you outside to play

There is a new kid in town

Who lives on your block

And she's just a hop, skip, and jump away.

Little Lizzy is her name

And she just has one favorite game.

It's called swing the bloody ax

And see your family run

Doesn't that sound

Oh, so fun.

She tried playing it with her dad

But he was too tired and that made her mad

So, Little Lizzy swung anyway

Ending his nap

As his life drained away.

After knocking him down

A bloody notch of Ew

She then asked her mom

To play the game too.

It was then Lizzy realized

She was no longer blue

While swinging the ax

Forty times through.

As she sat all alone

Pondering her slaughter

Your knock on the door

Made her thoughts ponder

Who can that be

She shakingly said

It's your next-door neighbor

And his name is Ed.

And there shyly standing

On her front porch stoop

Stood a new friend to be

Of unfortunate fate

For you are now Lizzy's

Chosen play date.

For she needed a friend

A boy should do.

So, that is why

She bloody picked you.

The smile on her face

Said all that was needed.

As you walked right in

And quietly pleaded.

Do you want to play

And be my friend.

I'll be yours

To the very end.

And quicker than her ax

Slammed into Daddy's head.

I most certainly do

She happily said.

Just stay right here

While I say goodbye.

To those that are still dying

And whining inside.

After kissing her parents

Pulling the ax from the dead

Lizzy ran outside

Sending shivers of dread.

Her bloody new ax

With its fresh sharpened edge.

Was hungry for more

She laughingly said.

Let's go to your house

Are your parents' home now

I'd bet they'd so love

To see the girlfriend you've found.

Cause if we're best friends

As so you have said

You'll swing my ax too

Until they are quite dead.

Now we both shall see

Lizzy giggles with glee

As she knocks on their door

Yelling ring-a-ling ding.

She's looking at you

To tie up the score

While your Mommy and Daddy

Stand in Abhor

Because that's what best friends

Are Bloody made for.

Lizzy's favorite game

You both now shall play.

If not for tomorrow

It will so be today.

Now swing her bloody ax

And see your family run.

Doesn't that sound

Oh, so fun.

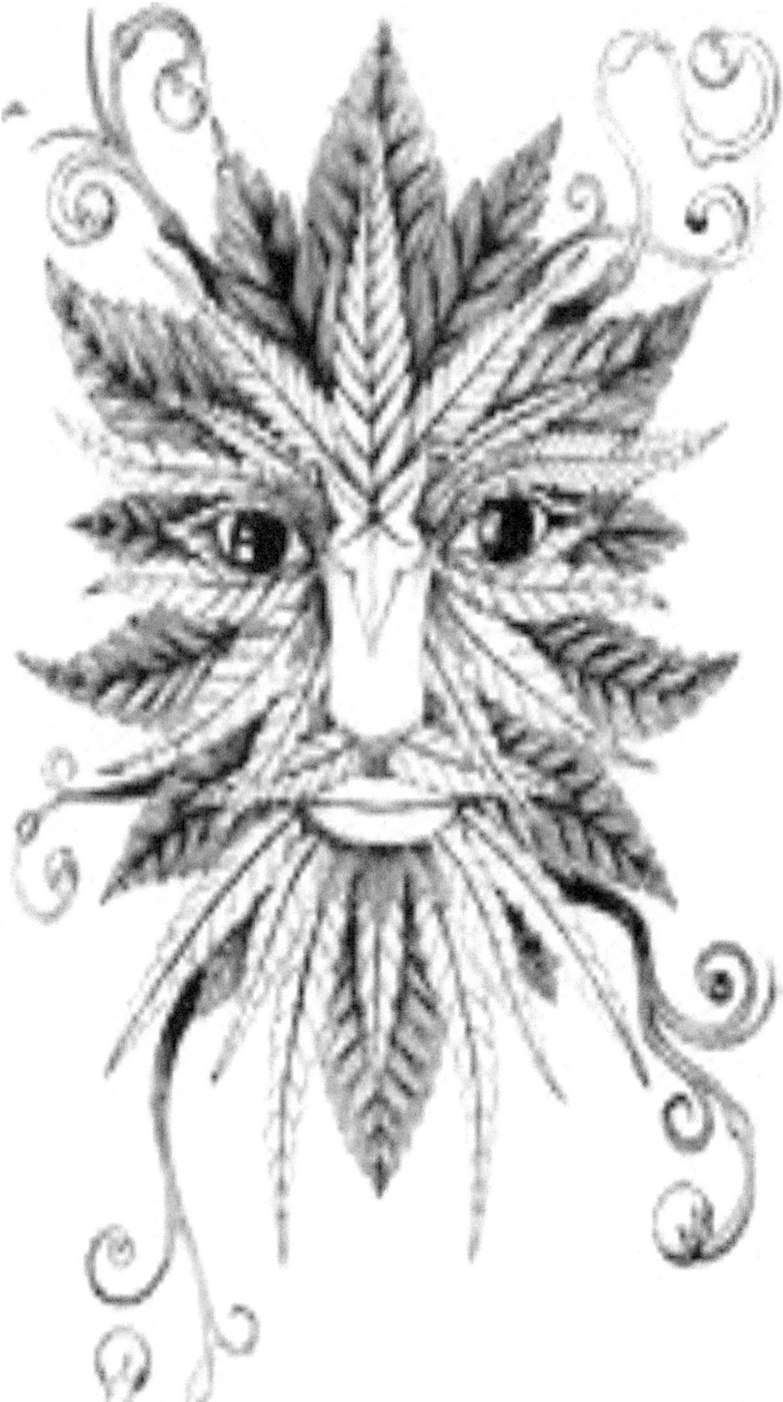

QUOTES FROM THE GREENMAN.

Never ask a spirit to cross their fingers

And solemnly swear.

They Can't.

Their Ghost!

Don't let the Bedbugs Bite 2
Critters, Jitters, & Shivers

E.A. Green

86

Welcome home my Monstrous Friends.

Did you feed your hidden Addam's in the Greenman's

Don't' Let The Bedbugs Bite 1.

Then you're going to

Glutton your soul on

Don't Let The Bedbugs Bite 2.

Critters, Jitters, and Shivers.

This Photo by Unknown Author is licensed under CC BY-SA-NC

TABLE OF CONTENTS.

QUOTES FROM THE GREENMAN.

WORRY WART.

QUOTES FROM THE GREENMAN.

THE MAW MAN.

QUOTES FROM THE GREENMAN.

ROLLIE POLLIE.

QUOTES FROM THE GREENMAN.

MOLLY'S DOLLY.

QUOTES FROM THE GREENMAN.

CREEPY KATY.

QUOTES FROM THE GREENMAN.

ANTSY PANTSY.

QUOTES FROM THE GREENMAN.

SCAREDY CAT.

QUOTES FROM THE GREENMAN.

TEETHING TINY.

QUOTES FROM THE GREENMAN.

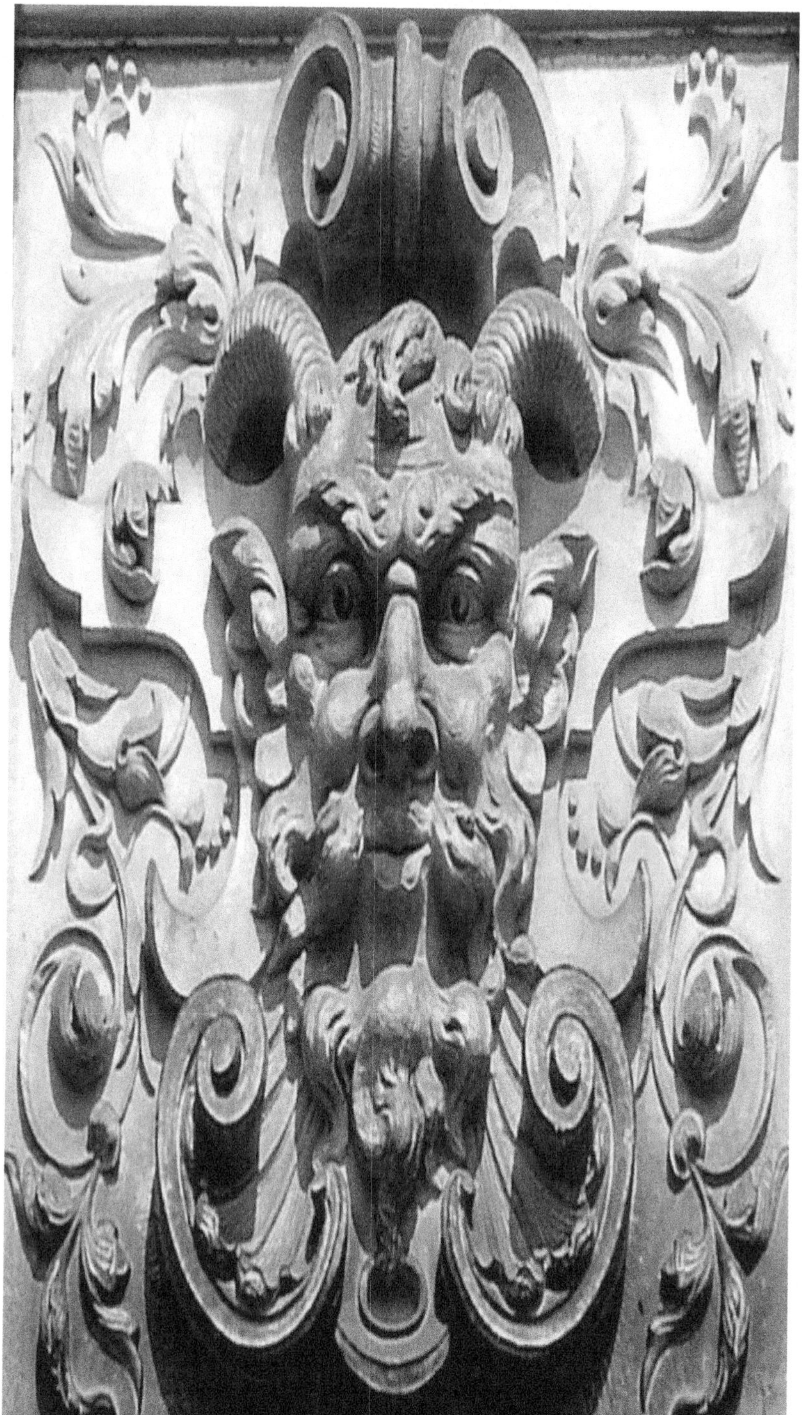

QUOTES FROM THE GREENMAN.

A fake friend just takes.

A family friend just needs.

But, the friends who ask you

To help bury a body

Are your Best Friends Truly.

Always.

Indeed.

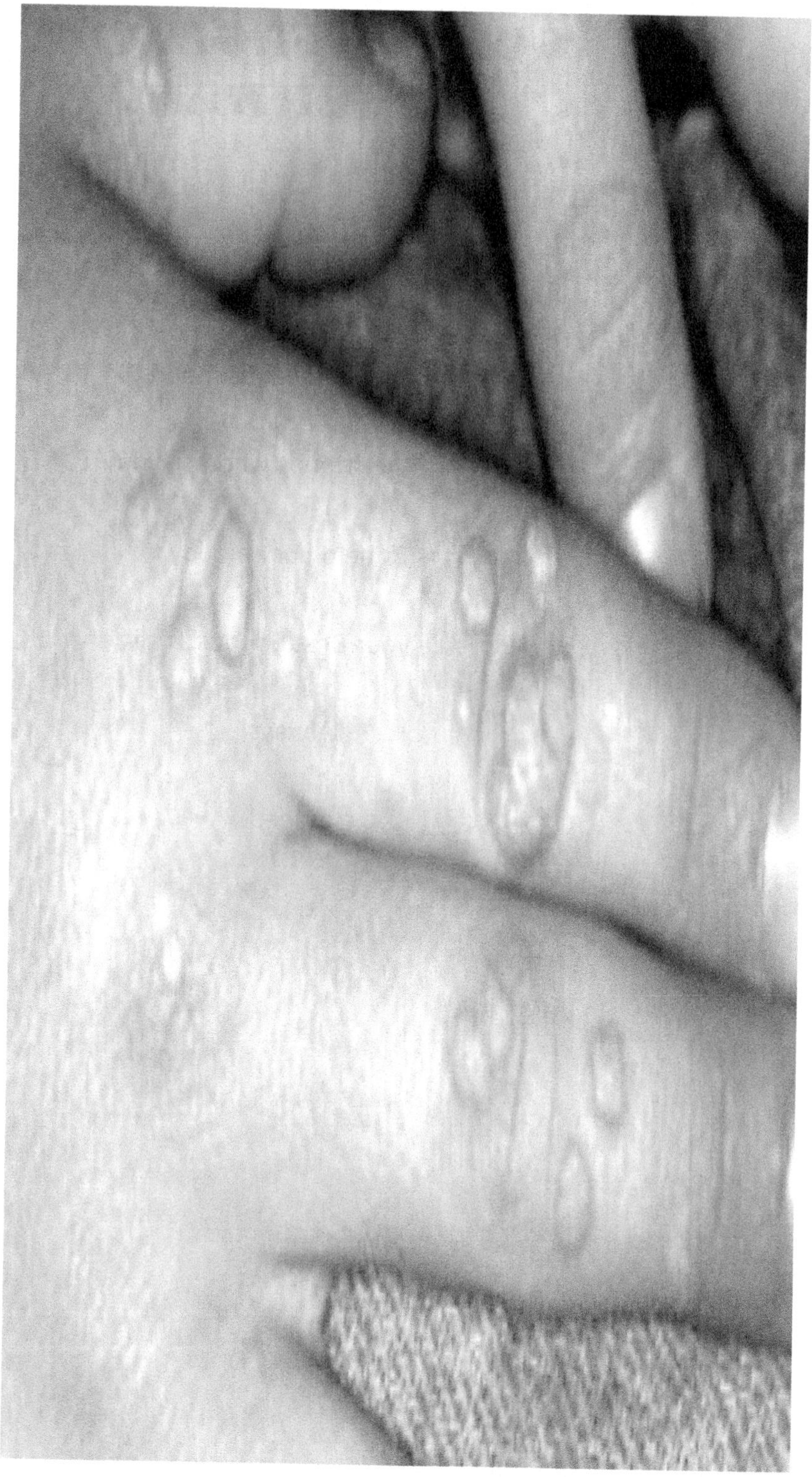

WORRY WART.

There are many things to daunt about

In your sleeping room.

Georgy's in the closet

While Eddie Bears near you.

Mr. Blister wants to be fed

And Bloody Mary desires you dead.

So, try not to worry

Your sweet little head

Or there will come

A wart instead.

It'll be on the hand.

Fingertip too.

Maybe elsewhere?

Upon your who knew.

Now, Lizzy's outside

Wanting to play.

The Hellhounds do too

As their howls do fray.

Thankfully, her sharpened ax

Keeps them at bay.

So, try not to worry

Your sweet little head

Or there will come

A wart instead.

It'll be on the hand.

Fingertip too.

Maybe elsewhere?

Upon your who knew.

Now you can run

For the trees to hide.

Just remember who lives

In the forest these days.

For the Fairies are never

There to play.

So, try not to worry

Your sweet little head

Or there will come

A wart instead.

It'll be on the hand.

Fingertip too.

Maybe elsewhere?

Upon your who knew.

Now if you flee

For the house in dread.

There are places to hide

Besides under your bed.

Just not in the closet

Where the Maw Man is fed.

So, try not to worry

Your sweet little head

Or there will come

A wart instead.

It'll be on the hand.

Fingertip too.

Maybe elsewhere?

Upon your who knew.

Now if your pantsy

And feeling antsy

Rollie Pollie is the place to hide.

But, watch out for

His glutenous side

For he will swallow

Those hiding inside.

So, try not to worry

Your sweet little head

Or there will come

A wart instead.

It'll be on the hand.

Fingertip too.

Maybe elsewhere?

Upon your who knew.

And just when you think

Your safe from them all

Creepy Katy

Crawls across the wall.

While Molly's Dolly

Locks the bathroom stall.

So, try not to worry

Your sweet little head

Or there will come

A wart instead.

It'll be on the hand.

Fingertip too.

Maybe elsewhere?

Upon your who knew.

You now have

A choice to choose.

Be their friend

And not your brothers

Or you will Die

Like Scaredy Cat others.

So, try not to worry

Your sweet little head

Or there will come

A wart instead.

It'll be on the hand.

Fingertip too.

Maybe elsewhere?

Upon your who knew.

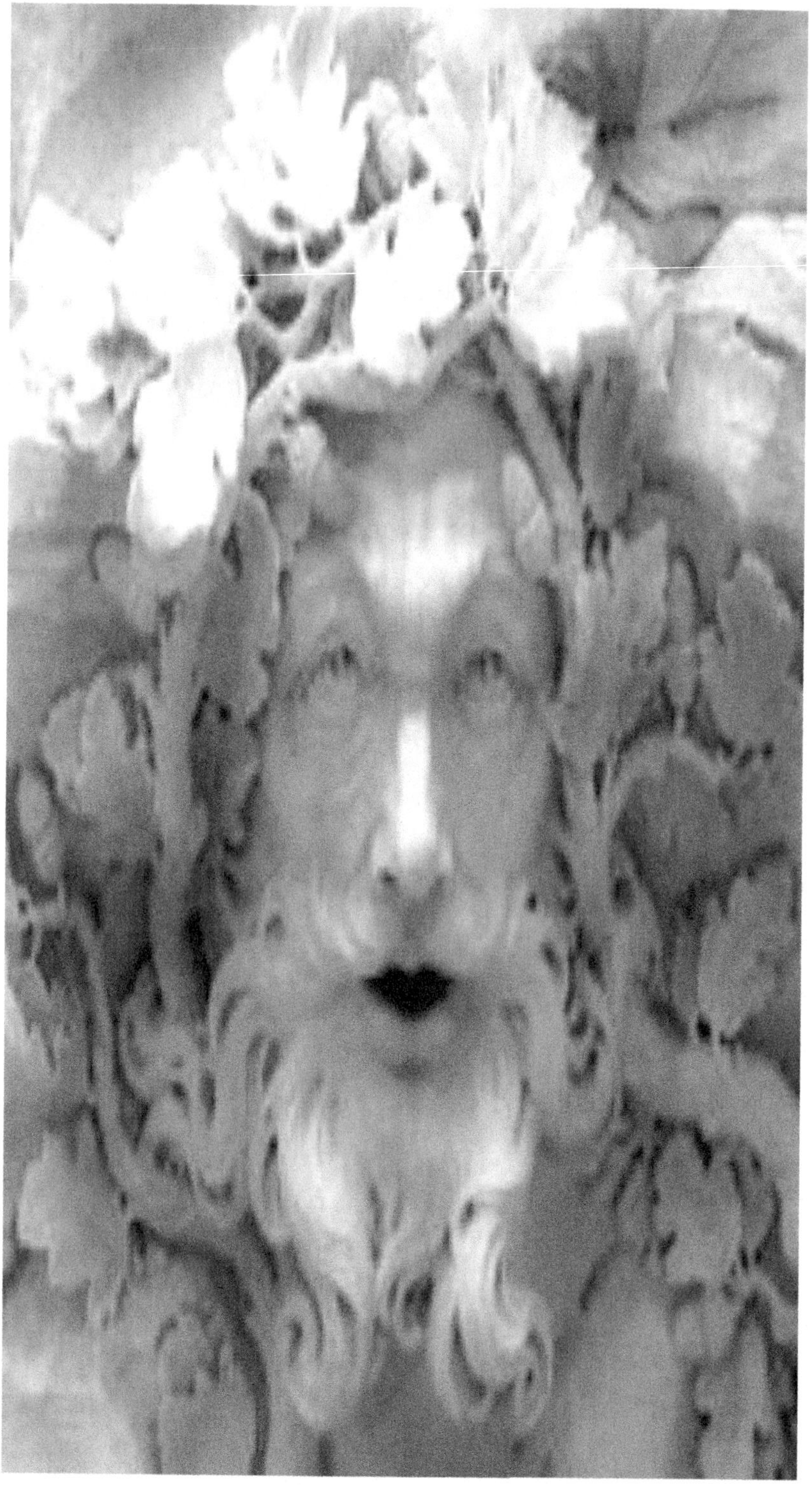

QUOTES FROM THE GREENMAN.

Why do people tell their secrets in a cemetery?

Because the dearly departed aren't listening.

And if they were,

Who are they going to tell?

Their Dead!

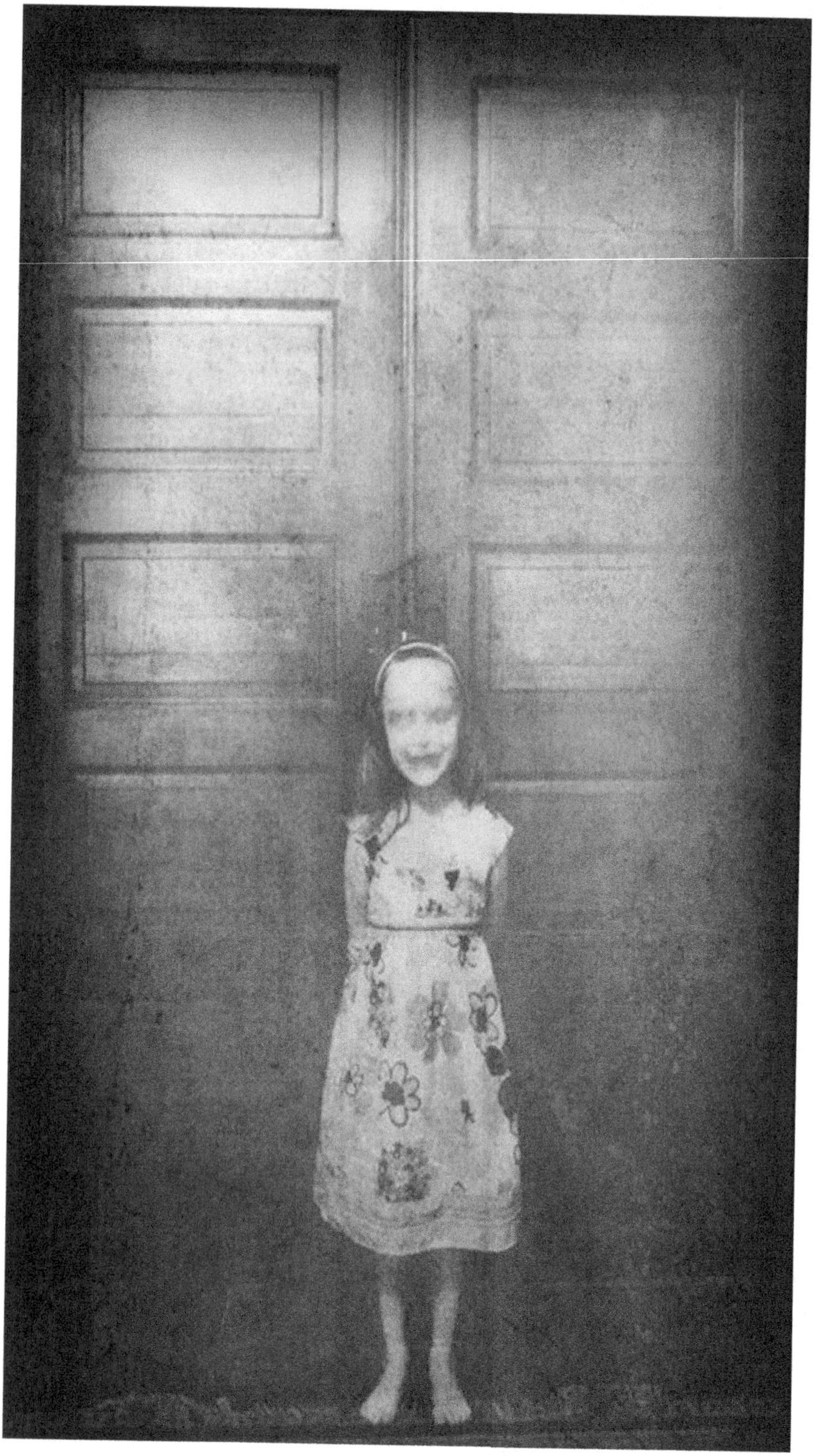

THE MAW MAN.

There are things in your bedroom

That live in your bed

But the Maw Man prefers

That you come to him instead.

You can hear his mouth open

When the door starts to creak

So, You Better Stay Awake

Or your soul will it take.

This new monster is a beast

Upon your flesh it will hungerly feast

But only after that last sneak peek

Making sure your fast asleep.

You can hear his mouth open

When the door starts to creek

So, You Better Stay Awake

Or your soul will it take.

There are things you can do

To keep him at bay

Like lock the closet door

Before your nightly pray.

You can hear his mouth open

When the door starts to creek

So, You Better Stay Awake

Or your soul will it take.

Now quietly do

What needs to be done

But, don't make a sound

Or a sneeze nor a hum.

You can hear his mouth open

When the door starts to creek

So, You Better Stay Awake

Or your soul will it take.

Now if you forget

To check it times two

Then always ask Mommy

Before she kisses you.

You can hear his mouth open

When the door starts to creek

So, You Better Stay Awake

Or your soul will it take.

The light is turned off

Your life within his chew

That's his chattering teeth now

And their chomping just for you.

You can hear his mouth open

When the door starts to creek

So, You Better Stay Awake

Or your soul will it.

Sadly, you didn't know

That's were Georgy lays his head

The latch he must unlock

Before climbing in your bed.

You can hear his mouth open

When the door starts to creek

So, You Better Stay Awake

Or your soul will it take.

As his hungry gullet widens

Just enough for you

It's best to heed my words

Before the Maw Man eats you too.

You can hear his mouth open

When the door starts to creek

So, You Better Stay Awake

Or your soul will it take.

114

QUOTES FROM THE GREENMAN.

The imagination is greater

Than the universe is wide.

Its depths contain more riches

Than the sea and all its life.

And if you try and silence that

Stopping its song and verse

You will miss the reassuring voice

Which softly values your worth.

So sit a spell and listen well

And let your spirit deeply inhale.

Those untold riches that surely dwell.

This Photo by Unknown Author is licensed under CC BY-SA

ROLLIE POLLIE.

Rollie Pollie

Bubbles and you

It's time for your

Bodily brew.

You'll hear at first

The Bathtubs thirst

As he sings

This hungry verse.

Now come on in

Little bee

Rollie Pollie's

Dinner thee.

His cold white shell

Is opened wide

Just enough

To slip inside.

So climb right in

Its playtime see

His stomach's full

Yet so empty.

You'll hear at first

The Bathtubs thirst

As he sings

This hungry verse.

Now come on in

Little bee

Rollie Pollie's

Dinner thee.

Your small frame

Will do just right

As the Bathtub

Swallows tight.

Now splash and play

Swish and swell

Upon his tongue

You taste so well.

You'll hear at first

The Bathtubs thirst

As he sings

This hungry verse.

Now come on in

Little bee

Rollie Pollie's

Dinner thee.

Now get all clean

And scrub there too

So Gorge Georgy

Eats not you.

Then when your done

Get out slick

Or Rollie's hunger

Will eat you quick.

You'll hear at first

The Bathtubs thirst

As he sings

This hungry verse.

Now come on in

Little bee

Rollie Pollie's

Dinner thee.

Bathtub Pollie

Will let you stay

When your done

But want to play.

Just know this

Before you do

Today's the last

Of your you who.

You'll hear at first

The Bathtub's thirst

As he sings

This hungry verse.

Come on in

Little bee

Rollie Pollie's

Dinner thee.

124

QUOTES FROM THE GREENMAN.

Even though pets are great to have,

It's best not to keep them inside.

Because if you do,

The cats will just end up trying to steal your soul

Before the dogs can let the Hellhounds in.

And never forget about the rats.

They bite too.

126

This Photo by Unknown Author is licensed under CC BY-NC-ND

MOLLY'S DOLLY.

Many, many lives ago, before toys were everywhere, a town's single doctor lost the only wife he has ever had and loved.

Stricken with grief; the father, to their one and only daughter, sought out the family's morbidly reclusive basement.

You see, He is, within a hundred or so miles, their only mortician too.

Seven days ago; his distraught wife snuck outside after everyone fell asleep and proceeded to do the unthinkable.

She slit her wrist under the Willow Tree out in the center of their remembrance garden.

But, that wasn't the end of it.

Something even worse than that happened to the mother before their daughter, just after sunrise that following morning, spotted her corpse from the opened window in her upstairs bedroom.

The beastly screams from the Wolverines were the cause to capturing the little girls undivided attention.

The violent carnivores where having a knock down drag out for those last few bites that were still attached and hanging on tight.

Three individual predators were fighting over who was going to succeed at finishing off the soft parts of her inner remains.

The Scream that rang out from the little girls horrifyingly shocked reaction resonated louder than the schools starting bell that was banging out its ten-minute warning about a quarter of a mile from the home.

It was also loud enough that it also got her father's attention down in their cellar.

Just as he busted out of the double doors that led below the foundations right-side; the hellcat's brawl over his wife's remains had sent the barn critters crying and fleeing for their lives.

The Mortician's screaming daughter seemed to have followed suite too, after he retrieved his gun and shot every last one of the varmints dead.

That was the last time she spoke or was seen by anyone other than her father.

Except for the funeral, three days later, it's been another four days since he's actually laid eyes on her himself.

Before his wife snuck out to do the deadly deed; she, earlier that morning, had once again miscarried another child.

Not only was that her eighth one, but it was their first boy.

The distraught parents ended up burying their one-and-only son under the Weeping Willow along with his seven other siblings.

After every death, the Salix Babylonica seemed to lose its leaves just a little earlier in the fall.

This year, its depleted foliage hit its peak the exact day of her and the baby's death.

July the Fourth.

A day that was supposed to be celebrated.

Something neither of them would ever do again.

Unbeknownst to his little girl, daddy, from a crack in the cellars outside doors, had been watching the child play out her sadness with stick figures made out of twigs, twine and leaves.

He couldn't help but to look in on her now that she finally found the courage to come outside.

The reclusive mourner really missed her presence and soft-spoken subtleness.

Out of the three play things, it was pretty obvious which one portrayed him.

Two of them had the fallen foliage, representing dresses, tied around their waste lines while the other was completely naked.

    She was replaying the fight they had after daddy refused to give into mommy's incessant begging for them to try once again because she was wanting to have another baby.

    This last one had almost killed her; and he wasn't going to allow or be a part of this next baby being the cause of her death.

    And that's when his heart truly broke.

    Their daughter was an only child and she was exuberantly hoping, "like her mother," for a playmate this time.

    But God, once again, seemed to have other ideas.

    As the Mordoctician watched her tears fall, his fell on the tattered piece of clothing he had just cut off from the bottom hem of his dead wife's dress.

    In his distress, the Widower had secretly dug up the old gals body that exact same night of her funeral.

    He just wasn't ready to let her go.

    And after quietly watching their daughter, she seemed to be suffering the same fate.

    They both missed and needed her.

Sadly, after the woodland creatures had their feast, there really wasn't much to work with.

Just to prop up her rib cage; it took almost an entire gunny sack of cotton to give her that full-figured look.

She used to jokingly tease him over how full of crap he was, when her charmer tried to fill her with bull shit for why he needed to go and trim up last week's haircut.

His all-knowing wife busted him every time.

He was just looking for an excuse to go and play poker with the boys.

And after years of their back-and-forth banter, her Mordoctician found himself once again shoving something down her throat.

Cotton.

Cotton.

And more Cotton.

But, today would be a little different than before.

He decided to take some of it back.

The father had a Eureka moment earlier when the Doc heartbreakingly realized that he has never bought his daughter a toy.

Not even a dolly.

Amongst the town, their family and what few friends they had; the grieving father was known as something else besides Doc, Mort, or the all famous Mordoctician.

Or Mordoc for short.

The sole provider for his family was also referred to as a tight wad.

He was a penny-pinching miser.

The running joke was that you could shove a full pound of bullion and a clump of coal up his butt and the coal would turn into a diamond before he ever shit out a gram of that gold.

And true to his form, buying a toy just to ease his daughters pain was nothing but a waste of good and hard-earned money.

But, there was something he was willing to do.

He fully understood how to stuff, sew, and dress a corpse.

And a dolly is nothing more than a smaller version of a person.

Since his wife had fallen on her back after willfully committing suicide, the animals had not been able to damage that protected part.

Taking the skin from her entire backside, Mordoc began to shape, fold, and sew the skinned remains of his wife into the form of a dolly.

He first created a torso, then added two arms and two legs before cutting off her hands and sewing them onto the doll. Then, before attaching a head, Mort pulled some of the cotton from the mothers cavity chest and proceeded to stuff his daughters new toy.

For that perfectly rounded shape of a head, he decided to use his dead wife's skull cap.

From the former housewives' eyebrows to where the neck attached to her cranium; the Doc, except for a circular patch of hair he left on the back upper portion of her skull, shaved, then surgically removed all that he would need for the dolly's full head of hair

He was very pleased with himself for thinking about using Mommy's real hair instead of cutting up one of his wigs.

Those were needed for the grandmas who were unlucky enough to have theirs thrown away at the hospital.

Once they were dead, their grimy wigs were considered Bio Hazards and were not allowed to accompany them into the afterlife.

And at the family's requesting, the makeshift coroner didn't always follow that rule.

He dropped one once that had so much hair spray on it, that the damned thing actually cracked his toe from the gallons of Aqua Spray that had been pumped upon it.

It weighed a good five pounds if not more.

The eight-inch shoulder length cut he left on his wife's hair piece would make the perfect length for Molly's Dolly.

Just like his former wife's hair style, it stretched all the way down to the dolls rear waist.

After admiring his perfectly stitched work, and making sure that the dolly was pleasantly plump, Mort the Miser decided to save even more money and quickly fixed on using the Boatman's two coins as the dolly's eyes.

He just needed to pierce the copper pennies before sewing them on first.

Then, using a scrapped piece of his dead wife's garment, the little girls Doctor Daddy began to create the most beautiful dress he has ever sewn.

Like her mother's, it would have linings, hems, buttons, and bows.

All the things little girls liked, he supposed.

    The rest of mommy's dress would be put to good use on the next Jane Doe that just happened to roll through the cellars double doors.

    As his nimble fingers worked away; so did pretty much the rest of their day.

    It wasn't until Molly banged on the door for dinner, right at his last sewing stitch, that it suddenly dawned on him just how late it actually was.

    Thankfully, he had gotten it done.

    Molly had a dolly.

    Now, you would think that this is where their story would just happily end.

    But, you would be wrong.

    And this is what the town soon said, after she too was positively pronounced dead.

Mother Dolly talked to Molly

Telling her what to do.

When their baby's

Fuss and cry

    Be real quiet

When walking by

And leave your dolly

So they can die.

   The last persons to find Molly's Dolly was right before she died during her ninety-second birthday.

   It was a couple who had gone to the nursing home to show off their new baby to her Great, Great Grandmother.

   The dolly was never again seen after their unlucky visit.

   "The rumor was," everything belonging to the baby had been donated to an unknown thrift store after it passed away.

   Molly's Dolly was gone for good.

   Or, was it?

   Out of all the stuffed toys in your room; do you know where your Dollies come from?

   I suggest you check before Mother Dolly talks to you.

   Or, you may end up quite dead too.

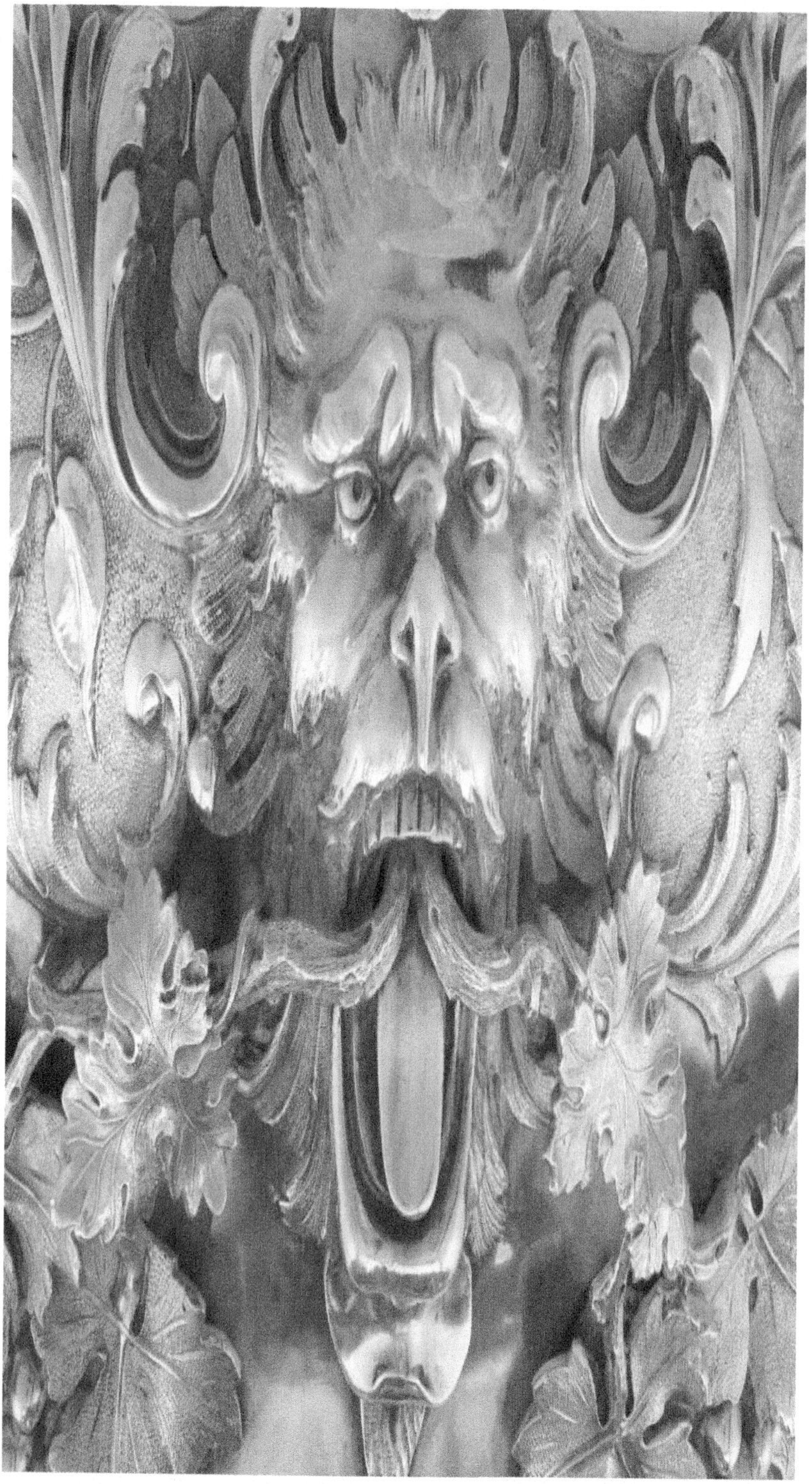

QUOTES FROM THE GREENMAN.

Don't let your life

Fall to the floor.

Don't let your life

Walk out the door.

Pick up your life

And value its worth.

Pick up your worth

And value its life.

This will happen

The moment you see.

That happiness is something

You must work to achieve.

140

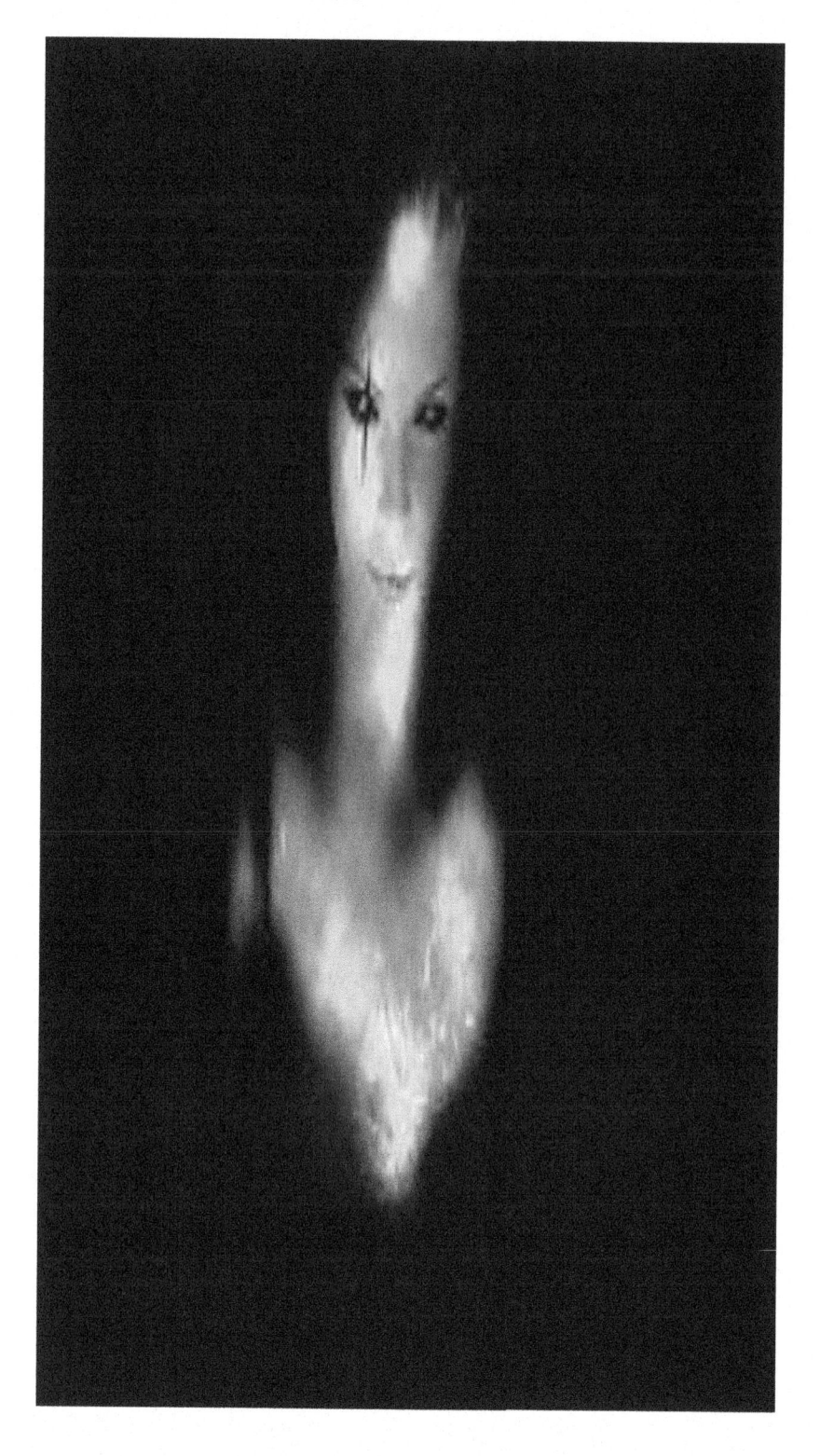

CREEPY KATY.

If your craving

For some hexing and vexing

Then katy's the one

You should be texting.

She has potions and spells

Bubbles and brews

And tons of dolls

For some who-do voodoo.

All this she has

And other things too

When the urge to curse

Comes upon you.

And if you need more

For something abhor

Her cemetery is open

Always past four.

Just quietly knock

On the Mausoleums door

Making sure not to wake

The dead on her floor.

All this she has

And other things too

When the urge to curse

Comes upon you.

She's grinding their bones

For your elixir powder

Will you look at the time

It's the exact witching hour.

Now all things are well

As she spouts out a spell

A love potion for two

For you and your beau.

All this she has

And other things too

When the urge to curse

Comes upon you.

Now if you came

With evil intentions

The Voodoo Queen

Will change who's she's Hexing.

So try not to scream

While its poured down your throat

And try not to cry

As Katy takes what she wants.

All this she has

And other things too

When the urge to curse

Comes upon you.

The wedding is set

Till death do you part

You should have paid

And lost not your heart.

But, sadly you didn't

So here you both are

Laying your heads

In Katy's Boudoir.

All this she has

And other things too

When the urge to curse

Comes upon you.

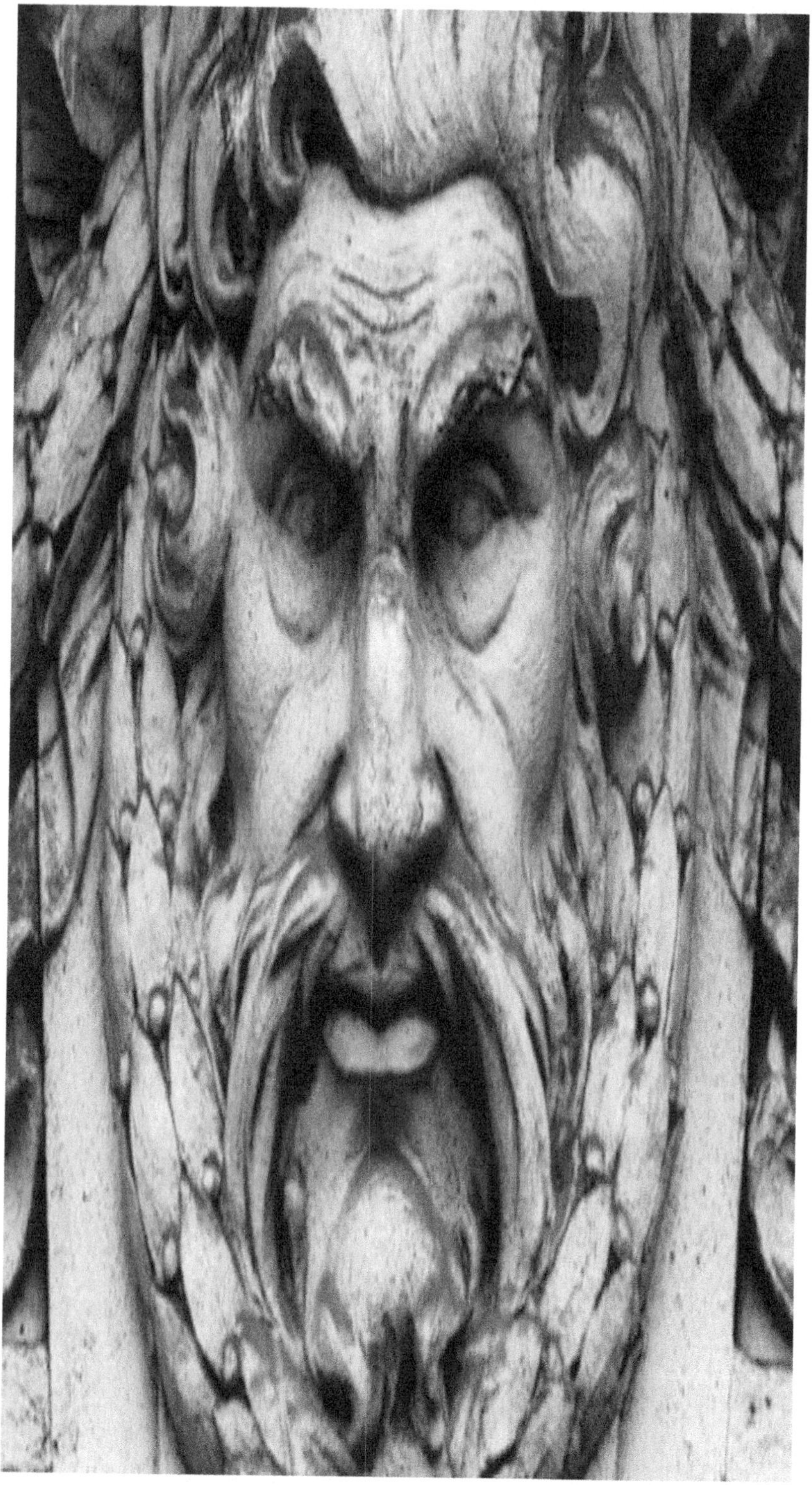

QUOTES FROM THE GREENMAN.

A fake friend just shows you

His locked box of torture devices.

A true friend gives you the key

And expects you to play with them.

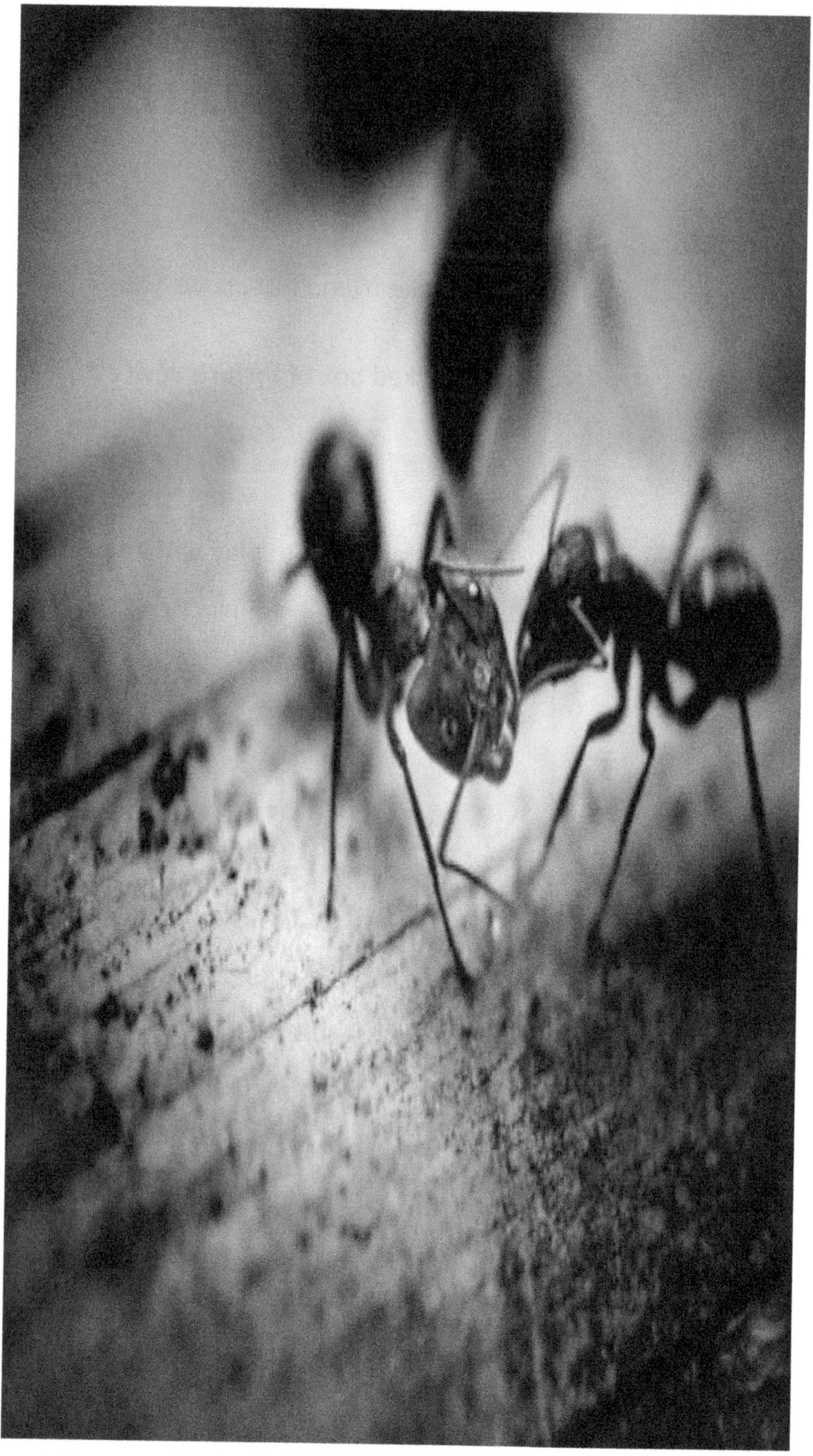

ANTSY PANTSY.

There are many things to hear

And so much to fear

When the Bedbugs start to creep

After your parents go to sleep.

So, what are you to do

When all alone at night

With nowhere to run

And filled with Horrid Fright.

I highly suggest

You listen oh so well

As your Antsy Pantsy rings

Its deadly rattling bell

Or, on this night

Your lonesome soul will Wail.

So, before the creeps

Begins to prey

Upon your thoughts and dreams.

Gather up

And put outside

This deadly mix that be.

Scaredy Cat.

Eddie Bear,

And Molly's Dolly three.

I highly suggest

You listen oh so well

As your Antsy Pantsy rings

Its deadly rattling bell.

Or, on this night

Your lonesome soul will Wail.

Now if you later shiver

Your backbone still does quiver

And then you feel a sickle

Causing your spine to tickle

Then followed by a hug

That makes you cut a rug

Your ensuing death

Is about to be dug.

I highly suggest

You Listen oh so well

As your Antsy Pantsy rings

Its deadly rattling bell

Or, on this night

Your lonesome soul will Wail.

You could hide in the closet

Maybe, under the bed

Or keep those covers tightly pulled

Over your scaredy head.

But nothing's going to stop

The fear and the dread

For the always hungry bugs

Find that which is hid.

I highly suggest

You listen oh so well

As your Antsy Pantsy rings

Its deadly rattling bell

Or, on this night

Your lonesome soul will Wail.

Now if you feel a leg

And there's more than a few

Then you sense his prickly hair

And sharpened fangs too

Followed by its many eyes

All fixed on you

Georgy's severely hungry you see.

And wants to lick all over thee.

I highly suggest

You listen oh so well

As your Antsy Pantsy rings

Its deadly rattling bell

Or, on this night

Your lonesome soul will Wail.

Now the fun

Has just begun

Upon this night of fear

Because you left

Your door unlocked

The deadly three appear

Laughing at your screaming words

I WANT MY MOMMY HERE.

I highly suggest

You listen oh so well

As your Antsy Pantsy rings

Its deadly rattling bell

Or, on this night

Your lonesome soul will Wail.

If you want to sleep

Without all the fright

Run into your parents room

Where bugs stay out of sight

Crying, there are monsters

In my sleeping bed

Can I snuggly stay

Here with you instead.

I highly suggest

You listen oh so well

As your Antsy Pantsy rings

Its deadly rattling bell

Or, on this night

Your lonesome soul will Wail.

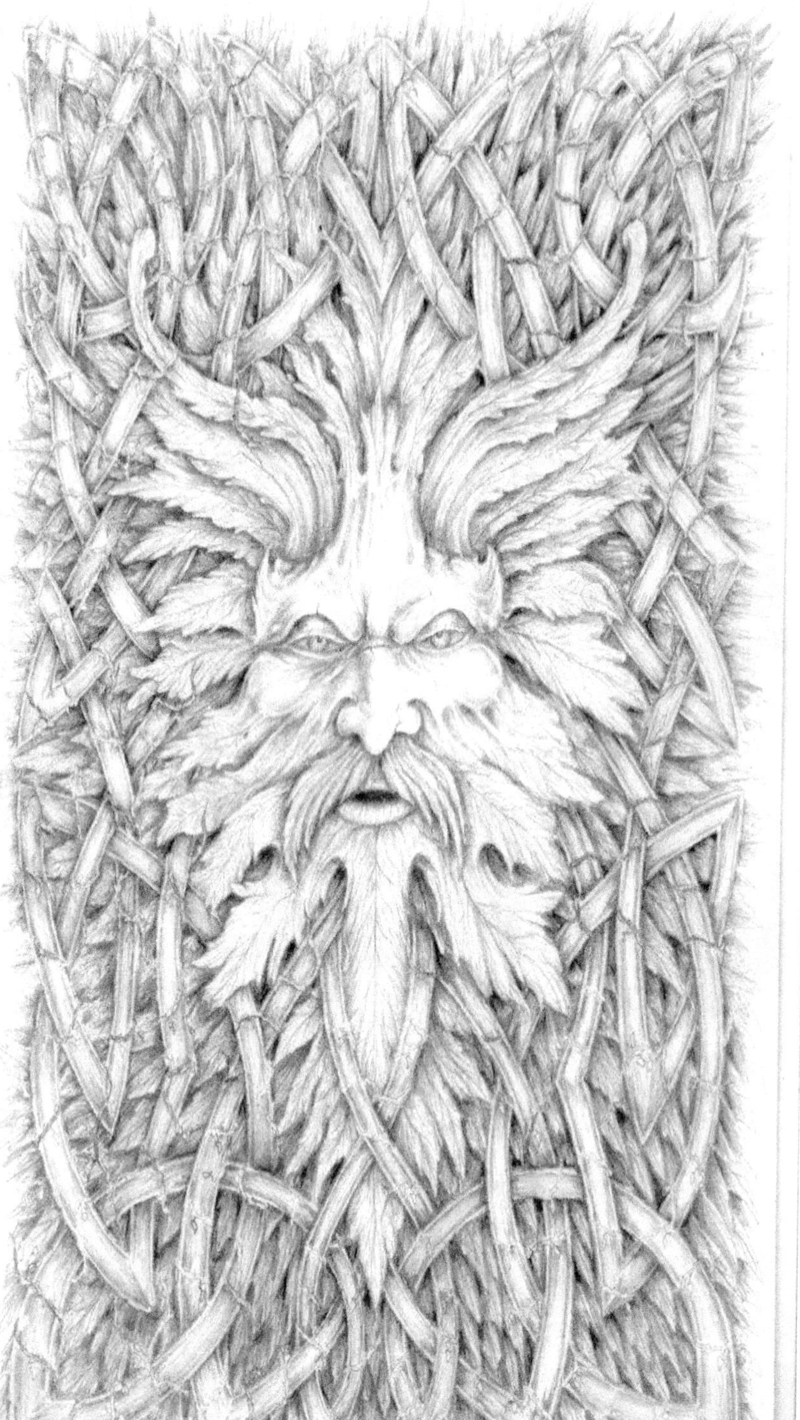

QUOTES FROM THE GREENMAN.

Fly my friends

And dance with glee.

Make your joy

For all to see.

And if others frown

To bring you down.

There's only one thing

That'll turn them around.

Sing Real Loud

Come Soar With Me!

And be my friend

For eternity.

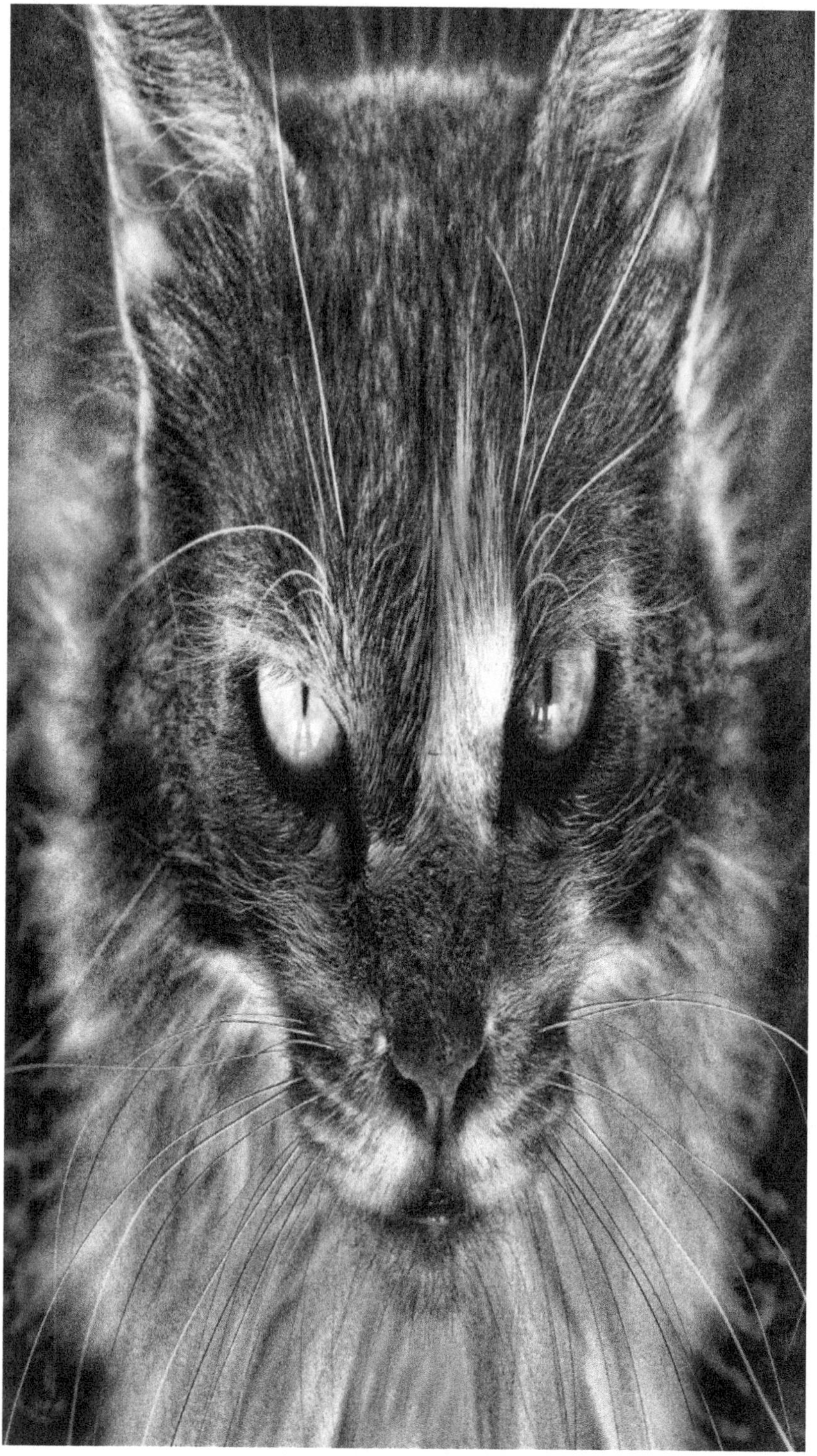

SCARDEY CAT.

If your cats a scaredy

Fraidy

And shuns

When things unseen

Cause things undone.

Then I warningly suggest

That you

Run.

Run.

Run.

When the shadows creep

Across a well-lit floor

And something then bumps

Against your opened door

What do you do

When the cat wants no more

Do you stay and play

Or follow its abhor.

If your cats a scaredy

Fraidy

And shuns.

When things unseen

Cause things undone

Then I warningly suggest

That you

Run.

Run.

Run.

So, does it get your goat

When things up and float

And unseen stomps

Loudly kick and clomp

Do you duck away

Or just stick around

Searching for the noises

That went

POUND!

POUND!

POUND!

If your cats a scaredy

Fraidy

And shuns.

When things unseen

Cause things undone.

Then I warningly suggest

That you

Run.

Run.

Run.

If there comes a Monster

And a Demon or Two

But their invisible

Unseen to you

Its best that you have

Your frightened cat in view

Watching for its hunched up back

Your last and final cue.

If your cats a scaredy

Fraidy

And shuns.

When things unseen

Cause things undone.

Then I warningly suggest

That you

Run.

Run.

Run.

Cats are deadly too

As most of you don't know

They climb into your bed

Once you're snuggly dozed

Their one sole purpose

Is to steal your breath

Before the things that prey

Just for that sweet elixir

Which keeps them all at bay.

If your cats a scaredy

Fraidy

And shuns.

When things unseen

Cause things undone.

Then I warningly suggest

That you

Run.

Run.

Run.

Now when it comes to choices

The cat or them must choose

There is something you can do

Before your catnap

Slumber snooze.

Put a bell

Around Its neck

To wake you before its

What the Heck!

If your cats a scaredy

Fraidy

And shuns.

When things unseen

Cause things undone.

Then I warningly suggest

That you

Run.

Run.

Run.

To see the Demons you can not

Your breath the cat

Must snort and snot

Just wake before

They are done.

But look away

Before you do

Or, your life

Is all but through.

If your cats a scaredy

Fraidy

And shuns.

When things unseen

Cause things undone.

Then I warningly suggest

That you

Run.

Run.

Run.

There's Magic in those Feline eyes

Mirrors can they be

And if you look

Deep inside

You'll see the Things

That kill with greed

As your soul

Their hunger feeds.

If your cats a scaredy

Fraidy

And shuns.

When things unseen

Cause things undone.

Then I warningly suggest

That you

Run.

Run.

Run.

172

QUOTES FROM THE GREENMAN.

When life leaves you but two choices to choose,

Why not just flip a coin and see?

Because, Fate always needs a decision.

So,

Why not make it yours

Instead of hers.

Being an Adult means never expecting,

Or blaming,

Others for the life choices that are

Your Responsibility to make.

Not Theirs.

When you can do that,

You're on your way to greatness.

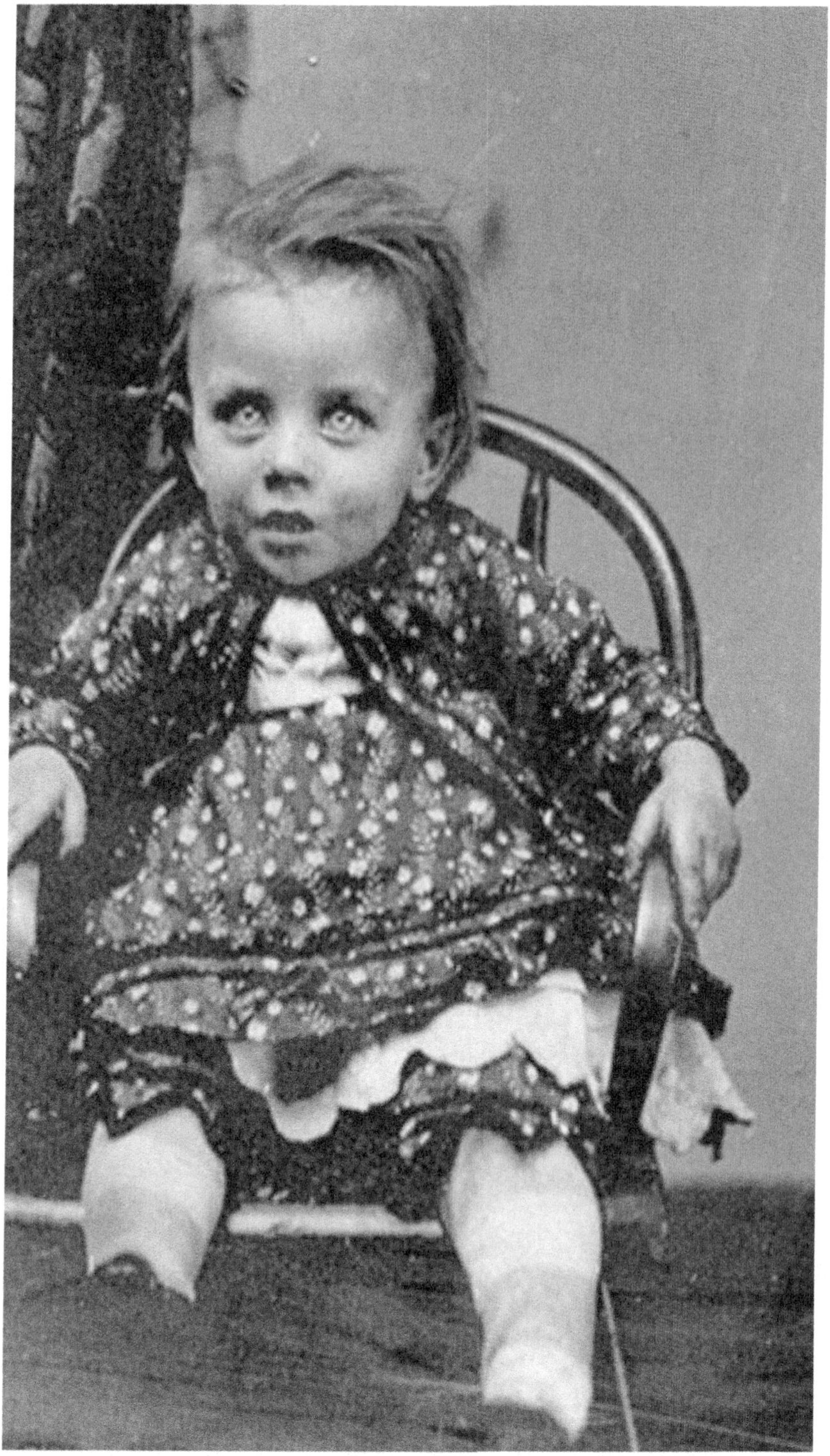

TEETHING TINY.

If you feel

The hunger start

And nothing taste quite right.

Try these things

He nibbles on

When Tiny teethes at night.

Some are Crunchy.

Others Goo.

Tiny Loves the Popping ones

When he

Chomps and Chews.

Before you hunt

And before you feast

Your dribbling tongue

Must start in the middle.

So hurry up.

And let's not piddle.

Some are Crunchy.

Others Goo.

Tiny Loves the Popping ones

When he

Chomps and Chews.

Now scatter the Critters

Across the floor

Towards the walls

And not the doors.

Grabbing and eating

As they fight.

The Creepies.

The Crawlies.

And those that bite.

Some are Crunchy.

Others Goo.

Tiny Loves the Popping ones

When he

Chomps and Chews.

Now,

This is where

The fun begins.

Feeling along

The edges

And corners.

Finding those creepies

Where they had crawled

Away from the lips

Of the never appalled.

Some are Crunchy.

Others Goo.

Tiny Loves the Popping ones

When he

Chomps and Chews.

The walls are next

Where some are vexed

For not all bugs are true.

A few of them

Have different things

They can jump and do.

They'll fly away

As you try

To catch and lick them too.

Some are Crunchy.

Others Goo.

Tiny Loves the Popping ones

When he

Chomps and Chews.

Now the ceiling is

A hard, hard place

Where you can miss right out.

But there is something

In the room

He can move about.

A jumping bed

For those that flew

To hoppity get them too.

Some are Crunchy.

Others Goo.

Tiny Loves the Popping ones

When he

Chomps and Chews.

Now here's a warning

To Tiny's friends

Playing in

His dinner room.

There are things

You must do

So he doesn't

Feast on you.

Always bring a Bug or Two.

Some are Crunchy.

Others Goo.

Tiny Loves the Popping ones

When he

Chomps and Chews.

.

182

QUOTES FROM THE GREENMAN.

The starting doors

To your young life

Are polished white and clean.

Unexplored.

Most unseen.

And ready to be gleamed.

So, remember to look

Where others won't face

To redeem the treasures

Of time and space

And then you'll find

Your rightful place.

Don't let the Bedbugs Bite
3
Ooey, Gooey, & Chewy

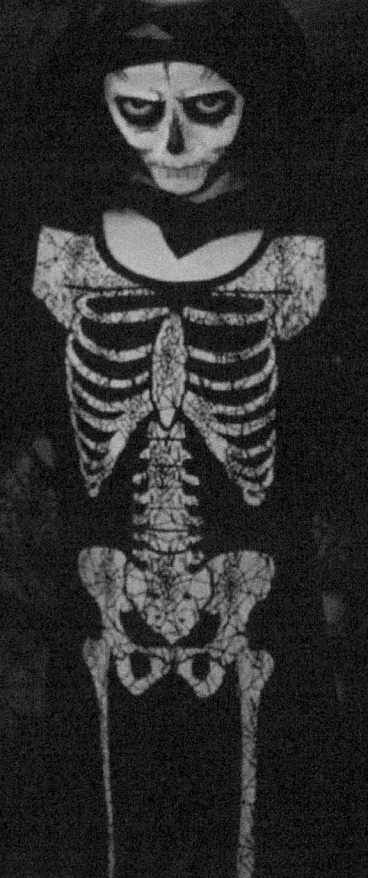

E.A. Green

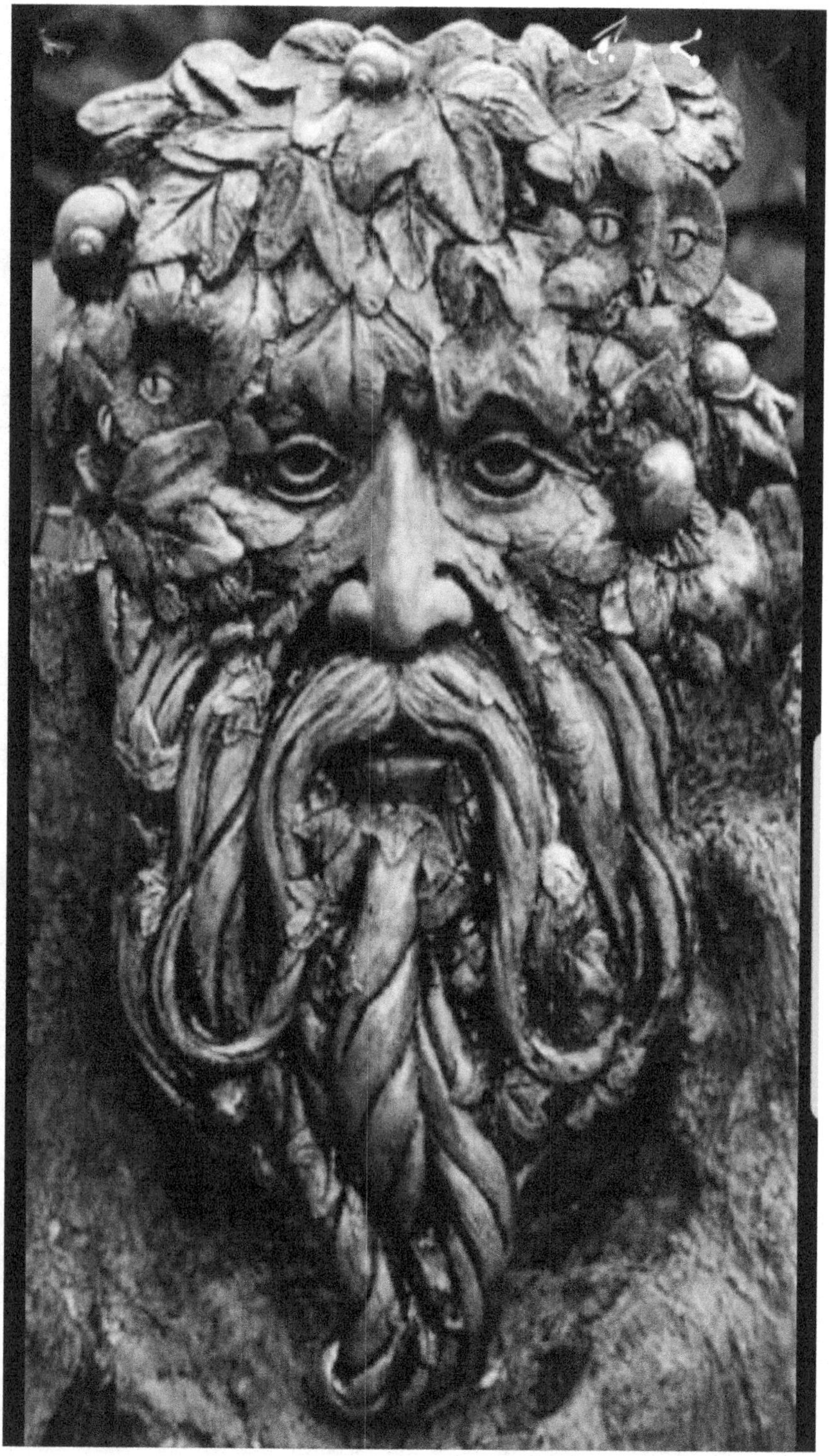

WELCOME HOME MY CHILDREN.

If things are getting stickily ickily,

You've slipped into the Greenman's

Latest masterpiece of nightmares and horrors.

Ooey, Gooey, & Chewy.

188

DEDICATION.

THE CLOWNS ARE MAD AT ME FOR NOT GIVING THEM THE PROPER RECOGNITION THAT THEY DESERVE.

SO I, E.A. GREEN, DEDICATE THIS MASTERPIECE OF THRILLS, CHILLS, AND KILLS TO THOSE WHO WHISPER THE DARK STORIES TO THE GREENMAN'S BLACKENED SOUL.

SHITS, GIGGLES, & WALLEY.

TABLE OF CONTENTS.

QUOTES FROM THE GREENMAN.

EAKIE PEAKIE.

QUOTES FROM THE GREENMAN.

LOUSED LARRY.

QUOTES FROM THE GREENMAN.

CHEWIE LEWIE.

QUOTES FROM THE GREENMAN.

SLOBBY BOBBY.

QUOTES FROM THE GREENMAN.

BLANKETY BOO.

QUOTES FROM THE GREENMAN.

SCARAB GARRAB.

QUOTES FROM THE GREENMAN.

EWWGARI BOOGARI.

QUOTES FROM THE GREENMAN.

WINKIN, BLINKIN, AND NOD.

QUOTES FROM THE GREENMAN.

192

QUOTES FROM THE GREENMAN.

If there are doubts about the right thing to do,

Think how you'd feel if others decisions were forced upon you.

And if you'd get mad or ticked from it all,

Why do to another that which would cause you to bawl.

It's better to pick up your brother,

And stand with them tall.

Then to attack their character

Which can cause them to fall.

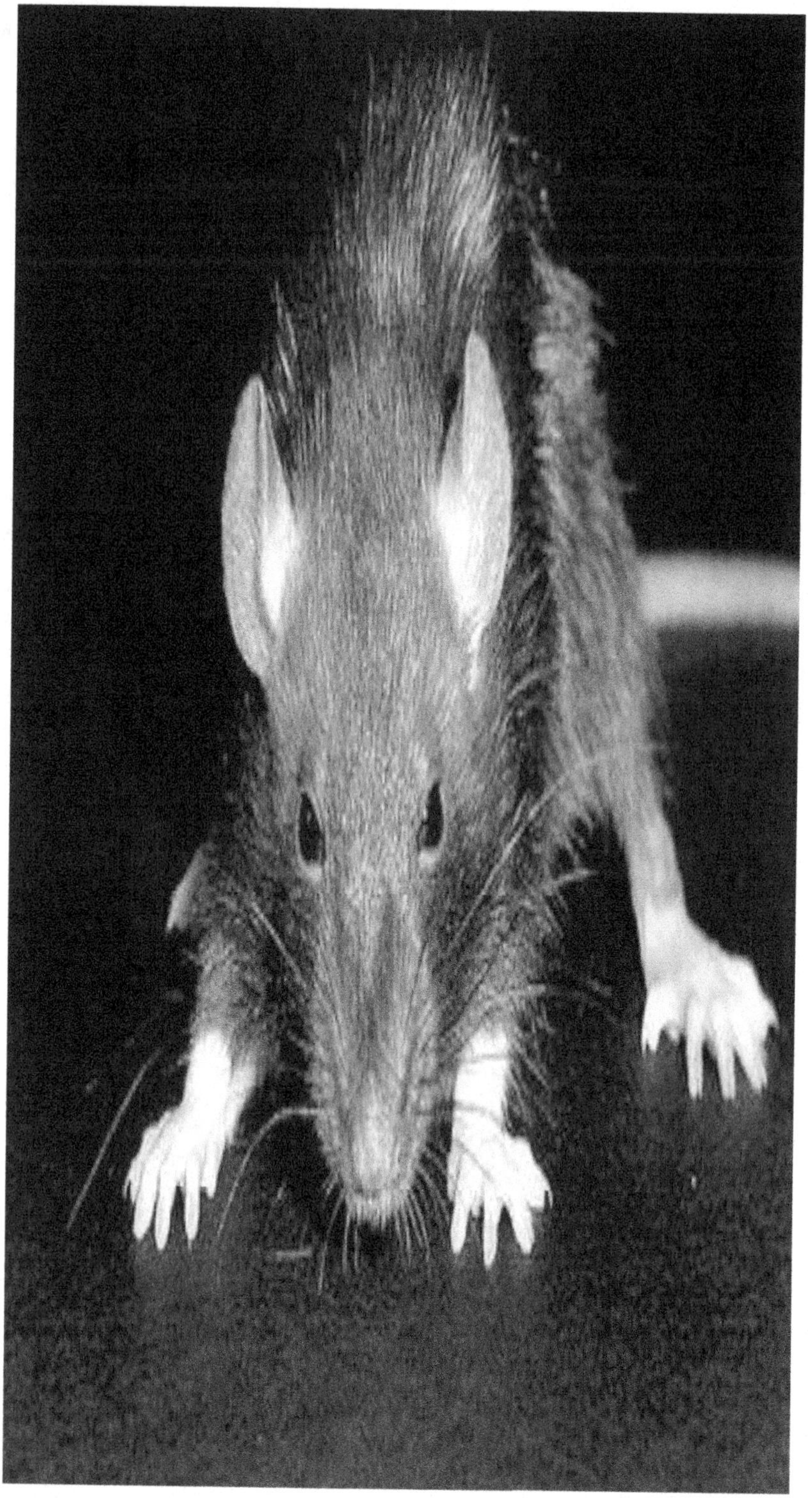

EAKIE PEAKIE.

You think your safe

Snug sound in your bed

And then comes the squeak

That causes much dread.

Eakie Peakie wants to eat

He's hungry to nibble

On stinky kids feet.

You'll know he found you

By the bleeding bite sore

You should have stayed

In the bathtub more.

Hear his nails scrape

Across the house floor

As he searches for food

In your dirty bedroom.

Eakie Peakie wants to eat

He's hungry to nibble

On stinky kids feet.

You'll know he found you

By the bleeding bite sore

You should have stayed

In the bathtub more.

The cookies smell good.

That sandwich looks great.

You shouldn't have snuck in

Your entire dinner plate.

Eakie Peakie wants to eat

He's hungry to nibble

On stinky kids feet.

You'll know he found you

By the bleeding bite sore

You should have stayed

In the bathtub more.

Your hidden pillow candy

Says take a chance on me.

Just sneak in the bed

After prayers are said.

Eakie Peakie wants to eat

He's hungry to nibble

On stinky kids feet.

You'll know he found you

By the bleeding bite sore

You should have stayed

In the bathtub more.

Now bubble-gum lipstick

Is a fun thing to have

Until you wake up

With no lips to be had.

Eakie Peakie wants to eat

He's hungry to nibble

On stinky kids feet.

You'll know he found you

By the bleeding bite sore

You should have stayed

In the bathtub more.

Now some people don't know

That rats love all food

Even the kind

Others abhor.

Eakie Peakie wants to eat

He's hungry to nibble

On stinky kids feet.

You'll know he found you

By the bleeding bite sore

You should have stayed

In the bathtub more.

Is your nose kind of runny?

Do you dribble while drool?

Are there crumbs in your mouth?

You're a smorgasbord fool.

Eakie Peakie wants to eat

He's hungry to nibble

On stinky kids feet.

You'll know he found you

By the bleeding bite sore

You should have stayed

In the bathtub more.

So, before you sleep tight

Brush those teeth well

And use only water

So your tongue doesn't smell.

Eakie Peakie wants to eat

He's hungry to nibble

On stinky kids feet.

You'll know he found you

By the bleeding bite sore

You should have stayed

In the bathtub more.

And if you must snack

On hidden food stash

It's best to do it

In a room you don't crash.

Eakie Peakie wants to eat

He's hungry to nibble

On stinky kids feet.

You'll know he found you

By the bleeding bite sore

You should have stayed

In the bathtub more.

Now before you sleep

The night away

Remember these rules

Which keep Eakie at bay.

A cleaned-up room.

A well washed bod.

A Non smelly you.

With a Winkin and Knod.

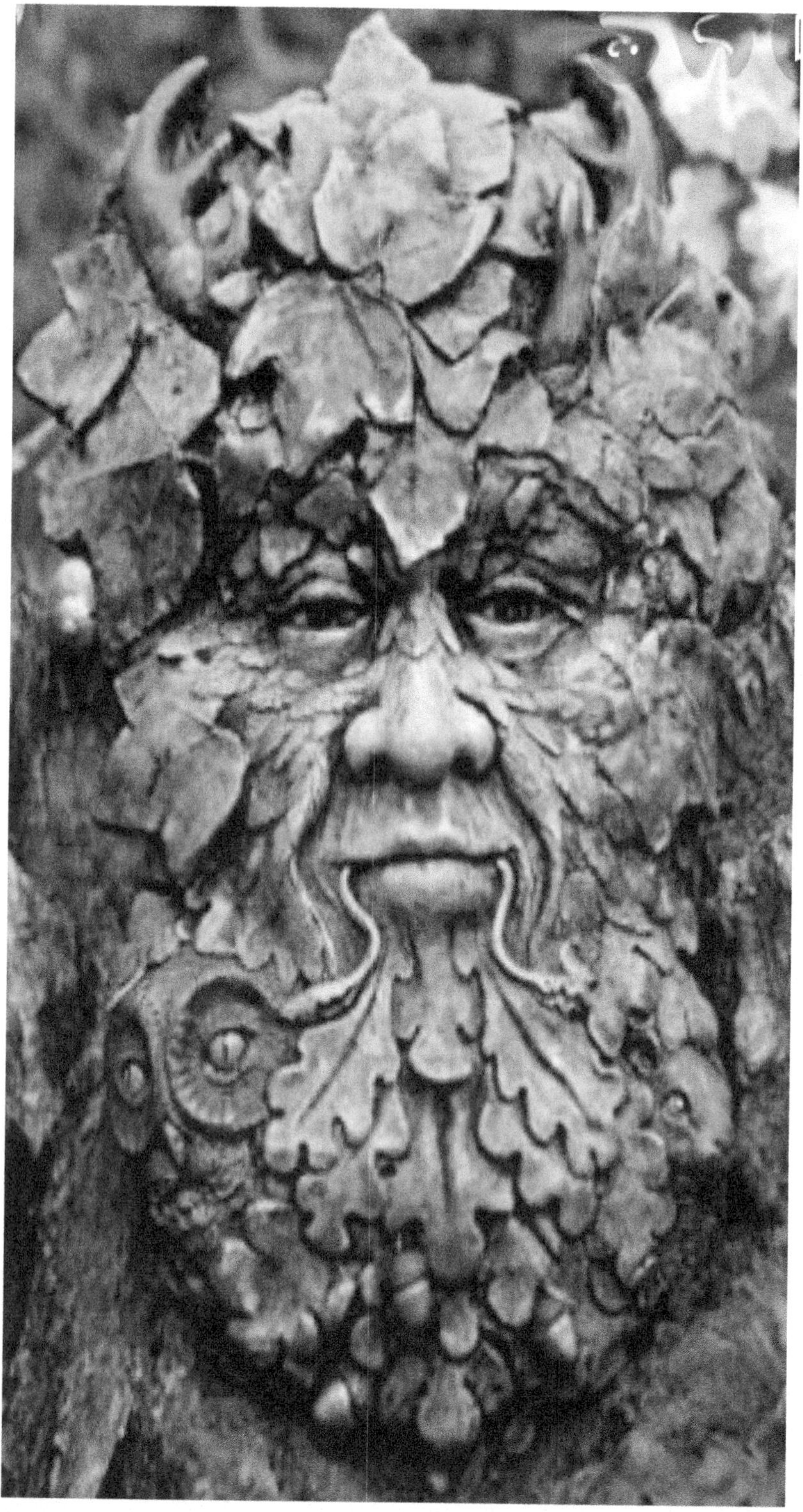

QUOTES FROM THE GREENMAN.

If you hear a creeping

And a crawling after bed

TURN ON THE LIGHTS QUICK.

You just might catch the monsters

At their favorite game.

PICK-EM-UP-STICKS.

They like to play it before using them

To pick, poke, and prod at their dinner

Before they begin to eat you.

206

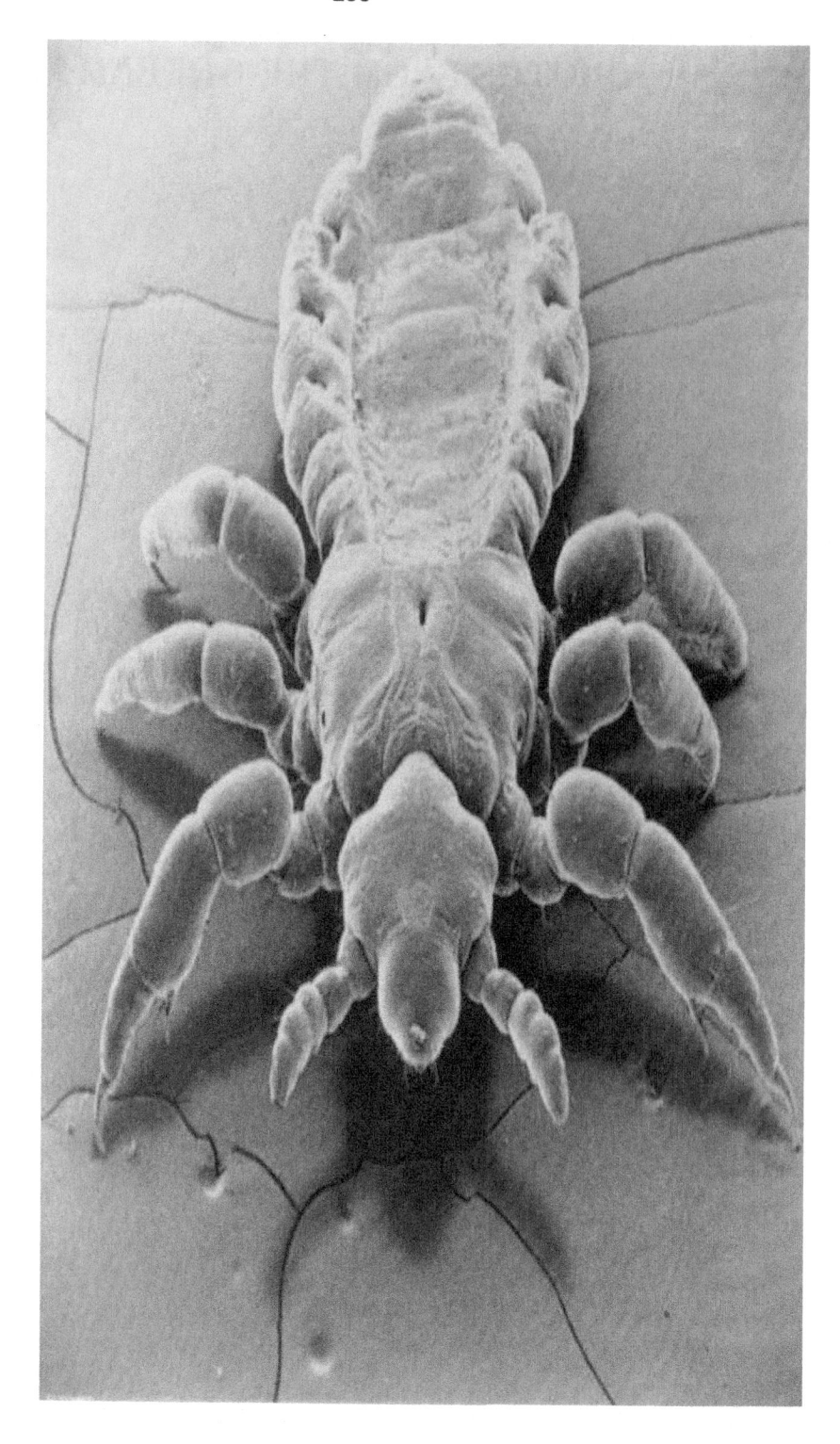

LOUSED LARRY.

Itchy.

Scratchy.

Bloody.

Ewwwwww.

Loused Larry

Is munching on you.

Six little legs

And teeth that bite

Claws that sink

And hold on tight.

Now Larry can't jump

Or fly around

He likes to travel

On things you've found.

Hair brushes

Hats

Scarfs and caps

Put them on

Or brush your hair

And Loused Larry

Will soon appear.

Six little legs

And teeth that bite

Claws that sink

And hold on tight.

You'd think he'd stay

In the home he's found

But he likes to travel

And get around.

You see his family

Grows real quick.

One times two

Then hundreds on you

All working to suck you dry

Digging for the brain

Before they die.

Six little legs

And teeth that bite

Claws that sink

And hold on tight.

Now the spider looking critter

Has no web to be found

But the sickly white dots

Say that he's around.

Your head will be itchy

Your skin will patch

As Loused Larry

Grooms his next batch.

And since the inn

Is now quite full

Onward to

Your friends must be

He wants to see

If they taste like thee.

Six little legs

And teeth that bite

Claws that sink

And hold on tight.

Now unbeknownst

To many sitters

In your bed

Is more of his critters.

Your pillow is

Home to many

And believe you this

There are plenty.

You see his family

Grows real quick.

One times two

Then hundreds on you

All working to suck you dry

Digging for the brain

Before they die.

So what are you

Supposed to do

To keep Loused Larry

From landing on you.

Wash your hair every day

And be real careful when you play

Keep others hats

Far at bay.

Don't brush your hair

With another's comb

And head scratching friends

Keep them away

Until someone says

Their safe to play.

All these things

You must do

Or Loused Larry

Will feed on you.

Six little legs

And teeth that bite

Claws that sink

And hold on tight.

Itchy.

Scratchy.

Bloody.

Ewwwwww.

Loused Larry

Is munching on you.

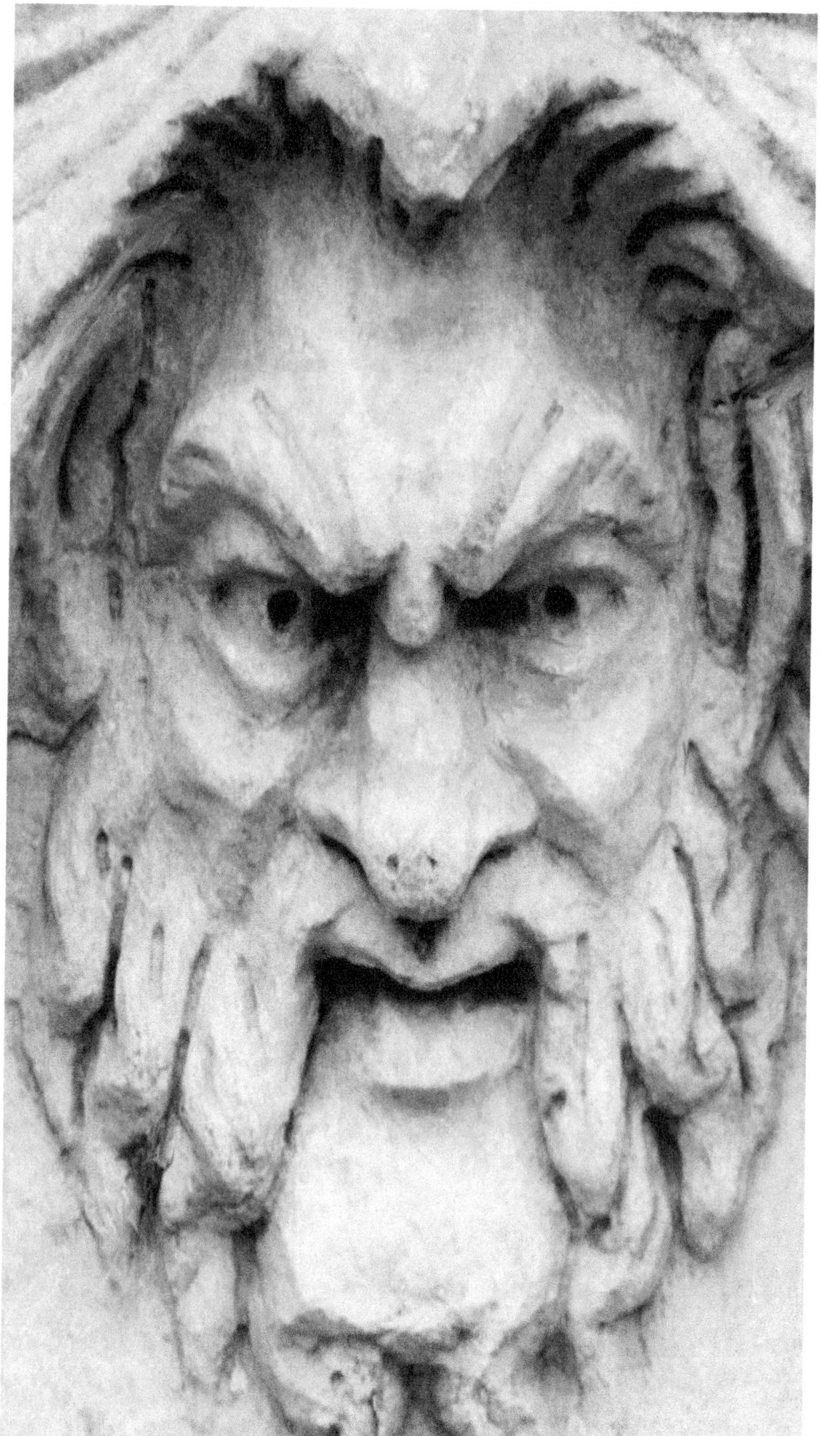

QUOTES FROM THE GREENMAN.

If someone slings a mud pie of hateful distaste at you

DON'T be that person who calls in the public

To witness the retaliatory issue you've now dressed up

Into a Three-Tiered Cake.

It's better to just pull out your easy bake oven

And cook the offender a piece offering brownie instead.

Blow holes are much easier to plug with food

Than trying to keep one shut with a physical shaming.

218

CHEWIE LEWIE.

When it comes to Chawing.

Chomping.

And a Chew.

Little Roach Lewie

Has his sights set on you.

You can hear his mandibles munching

Aggressively when he bites

As his salivary glands pool

While they sip

Drip

And drool.

Now the females aren't so bad

220

You can kill them with a swat

But Lewie is a boy

And that works almost not.

Underneath his exoskeleton

Lays a hidden vice

A set of wings

To fly away

So always swat him twice.

Another thing to creep you out

His six spindly legs

They itch

They scratch

And claw right back

To keep your hands at bay

That is why

It's always best

To let him run away.

But if you do

Remember this

You've now declared

A warring tryst.

Now Lewie is an eater

Of anything he can

From finger tips

To plump red lips

He even loves his spam.

And when it comes to darkness

Dankness

And night dew

If you've peed the bed

He'll always come for you.

You'd think this horror story

Would hopefully end right here

But unbeknownst to you

There's more than him to fear.

Two.

Four.

Six .

Eight.

Sixty-Four legs

And you're the bait date.

Twelve.

Fourteen.

Sixteen.

Twenty.

That count makes

More than one tummy

And you're so sounding

Deliciously yummy.

Thirty.

Sixty.

Ninety.

And more

His hungry family's knocking

On your alone bedroom door.

As you fall asleep

There's something you should know

They want to look you in the eye

So your lids are the first things to go.

Their angry and upset

You killed more than you should.

So, because of your hateful act

They've decided to strike back.

No matter the size

Or how long it takes to swallow

Cockroach bellies are never full

On your meat they'll wallow.

When it comes to Chawing.

Chomping.

And a Chew.

Roach Lewie's family

Have their sights set on You.

You can hear there mandibles munching

Aggressively when they bite

As their salivary glands pool

While they sip

Drip

And drool.

226

QUOTES FROM THE GREENMAN.

Did you know monsters have paparazzi?

They like to take pictures of their shocked

And soon to be eaten prey.

Why do they do this?

During the Celebration of Krampus,

They like to sell the funny snapshots as Holiday Cards.

Your last dying photo is this seasons

Most Sought-After Greeting card.

They found your distorted facial reaction quite funny.

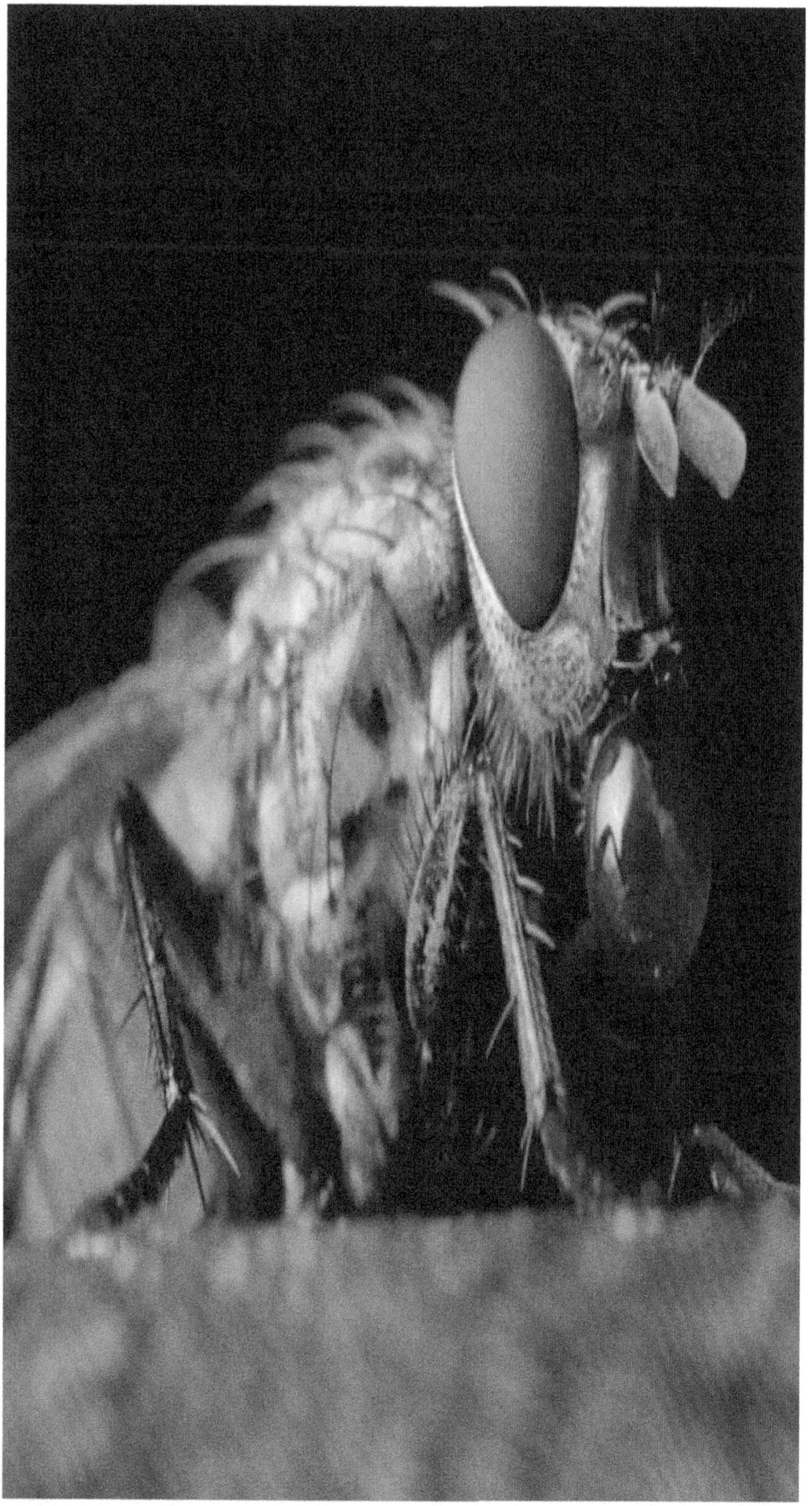

SLOBBY BOBBY.

When your feedin and drinkin

And hear a buzzing sound

You better cover that food

For Slobby Bobby's around.

There are also other things

You should always do

Besides that protective feat

Before you bite and eat.

Clap your hands

And smash him quick

But if too slow

You'd best just go.

Buzz away

Little fly

Come near me

You're gonna die.

Now Bobby's gross

He eats whatever

Never ask him

Feed me dinner

He'll pick the trash

As stop number one

And number two poo

Will make you spew.

It's big and brown

Sort of round

Runny too

No need to chew.

Buzz away

Little fly

Come near me

You're gonna die.

Now bobby's quick

And never slow

He dines in places

The living won't go.

So, hold your breath

Or you will spew

After you see

What's in his view.

Its bloated fat

About to pop.

Slimy green

And lots to slop.

Buzz away

Little fly

Come near me

You're gonna die.

Now for dessert

Your skins an oyster

Sweaty, unwashed, smelly bad

And there's so much

Too be had.

He'll silently land

Throw-up a bit

Then suck your goo through his maw

While his tongue licks it all.

Buzz away

Little fly

Come near me

You're gonna die.

Now Bobby has

A few bad habits

He gets in places

He shouldn't inhabit.

Your ear hole is

One place he likes

Your warm goo wax

Is honey times max.

And that opened mouth snore

Who could ask for more

A gluttonous feast

On unbrushed teeth.

Buzz away

Little fly

Come near me

You're gonna die.

Now the sad thing is

You might just kill him

And proclaim you've won the war

But horrifyingly and defeating well

His victory death rings a bell

It draws more like him in.

So, the best thing that you can do

For peace and quiet now

Is go outside

And leave a Pooey

Of

OOEY

GOOEY

And

CHEWY.

Buzz away

Little fly

Come near me

You're gonna die.

238

QUOTES FROM THE GREENMAN.

Even if it goes against all advice

And everything you know

Never be afraid to take care of you first.

NO!

MATTER!

WHAT!

ANYONE!

ELSE!

SAYS!

Sometimes, when it comes to saving our own lives, we have no other choice but to change.

And that's okay.

240

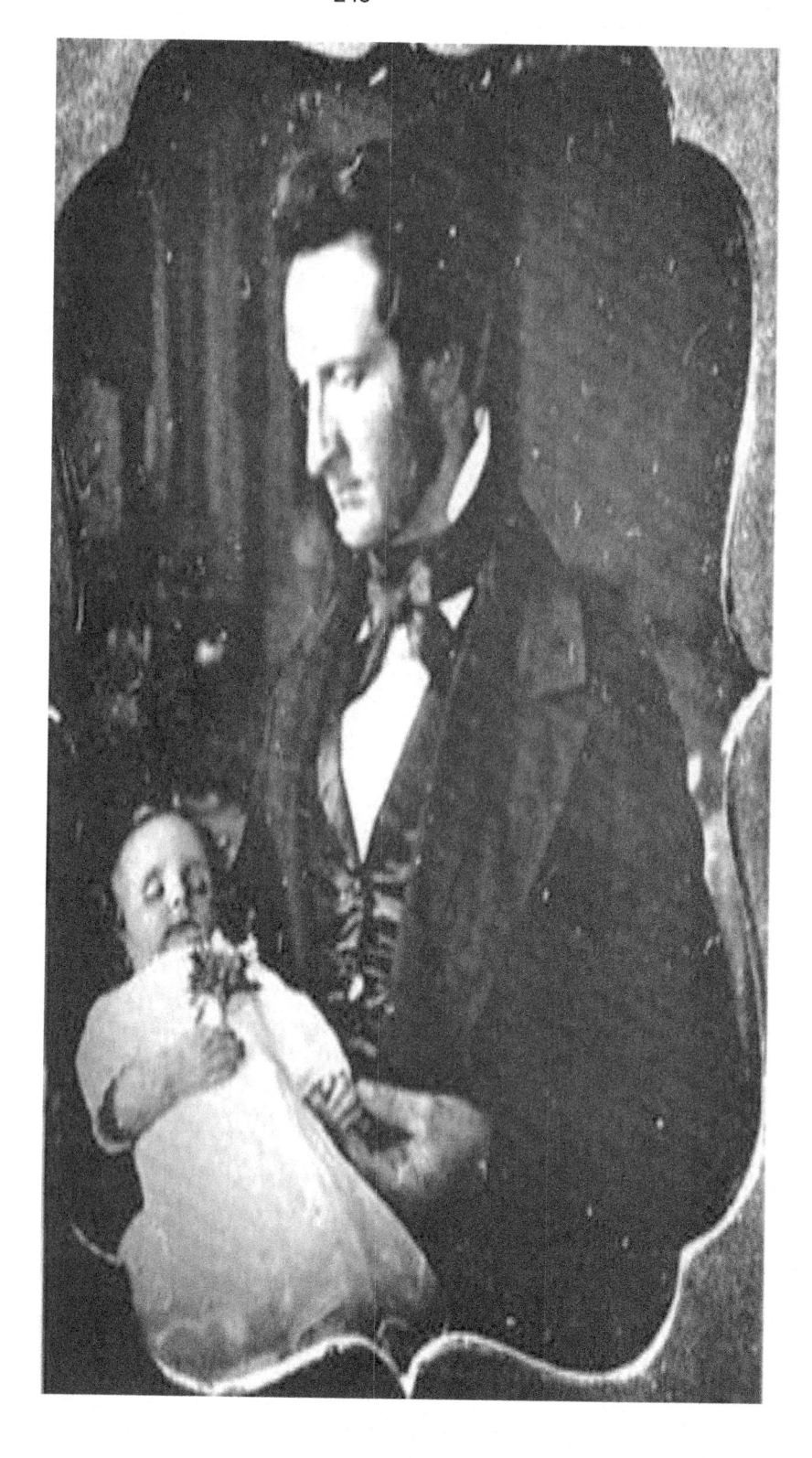

BLANKETY BOO.

Now, when it comes to urban legends; every civilization, every culture, and every history book seems to tell, "and sometimes record," these far-fetched tales.

But, are they really that far-fetched?

Most of us have heard about Bloody Mary, The Hookman who stalked lovers lane, Slenderman, and the one that, "To This Day," frightens every babysitter out there.

Especially if it's their first time.

Mam, the prank calls are coming from inside your house.

Now, I'm going to share a true event that has been kept from the regular public and especially a specific kind of consumer that likes to shop at specialty stores which deal with those one of a kind, and sometimes mass produced, items.

It's cursed retelling can only be found and heard around the campfires of those always on the move nomads.

Gypsy's.

This dying confession came from the lips of Lucia Kadilila, a pure, untouched, and unmarried girl of nineteen.

She shared it with her best friend Lavinia Codona before succumbing to the injuries that her boss Mr. Blackwell had beaten upon her after learning a horrifying secret.

The baby blanket that Lucia had been order to hand craft, had been cursed before being bestowed as a christening gift for his new born, and now dead son.

It all began the day he stood upon a table in the middle of the sewing room and announced to his workers that his newlywed wife was pregnant. And before he could be helped down, Mr. Blackwell just happened to notice a few things about Ms. Kadilila and her work area.

The dark-haired goddess was embroidering a baby blanket that he personally deemed A-Work-of-Art.

He must have stood there a good five minutes, watching her nibble fingers masterfully weave the most life like stork he has ever seen, before realizing that his trancelike gaze was now being met with one of her own.

And that's all it took.

She would be the chosen seamstress to create the One-Of-A-Kind blanket his child deserved.

She would also be the one who would end up being on the receiving end of his unwanted advances.

To make sure that his shenanigans didn't end up getting back to his wife and being the latest talk at the water cooler, Mr. Blackwell set Lucia up in a private office so that she could give her undivided attention to the specific qualifications that he was now requiring for this Monumental task.

His Baby was not going to be wrapped in a blanket produced by a machine.

Everything about his gift will be weaved and sewn by hand.

Now, "when it comes to Gypsy's," hand weaving amongst her nomadic people was a trait that was forcefully passed down from mother to daughter.

If it hadn't been for that other tradition, pre-arranged marriages, Lucia would still be traveling with the clan and not having to eke out a living working in a sweat shop in downtown Chicago.

There was no way she was going to marry the man her mother was indebted too.

Besides that, he was older than Methuselah.

As Lucia began her sequestered task out of the view of her fellow coworkers, she soon learned that being singled out by the boss is not always a good thing.

Between the jealousy, rumors, and special attention he was giving her; she soon became an outcast amongst company.

Even Mrs. Blackwell seemed to go out of her way so as not to have any kind of interaction with the seamstress.

As the young gypsy woman sat in her glass enclosed room, her question as to why she had been put in an office with a back door soon became apparent.

It was Mr. Blackwell's private way of visiting her so that he could grope and fawn over his future mistress without being seen. He had even tried to force himself upon Lucia once, but her knuckles forcefully cracking the glass for help put an instant stop to that.

So, as the days turned into weeks, and the weeks into months, the Four by Six-foot blanket began to take shape.

And so did the deadly curse that was being whispered, weaved, and stitched into every inch of its creation.

To keep her fingers nimble, and making sure the curse would stick, Ms. Kadilila dipped her fingers into a mix of her own spit, blood and tears.

She spoke sickness, heartache, death and insanity into every last fiber of that hand-woven blanket.

And the more Mr. Blackwell tried to take advantage of her kept away situation, the darker those venomous curses became.

When the birthing day finally arrived, Lucia was just finishing up with the hand stitching patterns that Mrs. Blackwell Demanded on being a part of the blanket.

She wanted there to be at least one hundred hearts embroidered upon the gift to their child.

And after soaking the thread in over a pint of her own blood, Kadilila spoke a curse into every last stitch.

Death, Hatred, Insanity, Wasting, Heartache, and anything else that a mistreated gypsy could think of as her heart began to harden and shrivel also.

It wasn't until Lucia's return to the threading line that the weight of Mr. Blackwell's abuse finally started to release its hold on her.

She even began to smile a little more when it was announced that the baby wasn't doing well.

With each and every passing day, the child became sicker and sicker.

As did Mr. Blackwell's wife.

She would wrap herself and the baby in the blanket and spend their days rocking each other to sleep as she cared for their sickly infant.

During this time, her boss was so entirely caught up with what was taking place with his family, that his unwanted attention seemed to become something of a past nightmare which Lucia actually thought she could finally take a breath and move on from.

But, all that changed once the boss's wife passed away about a week after their baby died.

He was looking for condolence and was going to use Lucia to get it, when he unexpectedly caught her in the midst of celebration and thanking her ancestral saints for answering her cursed prayers.

She was honoring them with praises for fulfilling the curses that were spit, spoken, and weaved into the blanket.

Lucia was also giving thanks for the unexpected gift that had been bestowed upon her also.

The death of the mother too.

Mr. Blackwell was so enraged that he dragged Lucia into the room where she had woven the death shroud and proceeded to pound out his anger, hatred, and authority in a way some women's husbands tend to do after returning from the pub in a drunken and sexed up rage.

And after taking her untouched purity, he left in a huff but soon returned in a puff.

Retrieving the cursed object from his office, where he had been keeping it as a soothing blanket to cry his misery in, Blackwell violently threw the death shroud at his new concubine and ordered her to destroy the thing the exact same way it had been created.

Stitch by hand sewn stitch.

The only instrument she would be allowed to use as she unstitched the blanket were her own teeth, fingers, and nails.

And as the unwanted physical abuse progressed from one day to the next week and into the following month; that baby bedding became saturated with her Accursed Spittle, Venomous Blood, and Broken Nailed Hatred.

Between her employers unwanted advances and the lack of proper tools, the unstitching and unweaving of the shroud took more than six months. Approximately one hundred and eighty-three days passed before those last pieces of thread were finally pulled apart.

Laying at Lucia's feet were hundreds of yards of red thread that had once been whiter than pure, untouched snow.

And she had plans for every last inch of it.

Now that her boss no longer had a reason to keep her apart from the other coworkers, he no longer wished to look at the gal who was less than a ravaging beauty now.

He had destroyed her self-worth to the extreme that she quit caring about her looks, she stopped bathing, and she refused to change out of her dirty work cloths.

Lucia Kadilila was nothing more than an empty shell of herself that her coworkers could smell walking in the door before knowing she was even there.

Mr. Blackwell placed her at the far end of his factory warehouse so that he would never have to look at or smell her nastiness again.

She would be in charge of loading the thread spindles onto the machine that was used to spin the baby blankets that were being mass produced for the general public.

The haggard gypsy woman of nineteen, who now had the appearance of a forty-year-old, gratefully thanked those that watched over her as she proceeded to use that which she had been ordered to destroy.

She cut the cursed thread from the baby blanket into three-inch strings and slipped one into every garment the machine sewed.

There was approximately eight hundred yards of thread used in the blanket for Blackwell's baby.

That's somewhere in the distance of two thousand and four hundred feet of yarn she now had to work with.

By cutting it into three-inch slivers, Kadilila estimated that she now had the ability to curse almost eight hundred baby blankets.

However, if it hadn't of been for two separate instances, Lucia would have successfully fulfilled her self-imposed quota.

The number of reported dead from sudden infant death syndrome, all sleeping with a baby blanket from

Mr. Blackwell's company, "and his lust for her," put Lucia in the bullseye of her boss once again.

Unbeknownst to the company's employee, the owner had taken notice that she had finally started caring for her appearance and the widower was now hungering for the feel of his naked skin forcefully pressed against the Gypsy woman's once again.

And the day he decided to do something about it, the rapist unexpectedly walked up behind her just as she was placing one of the cursed threads.

The company's owner couldn't believe what he was seeing and hearing as she stitched that piece of thread into a brand-new blanket.

As unto the Blackwell's, so unto the buyer.

Let the curse of a Slow, Painful, and Wasting Death befall the baby and all those who purchase this and all other blankets.

That spoken curse was followed by a spit-soaked piece of thread being sewn into the garment.

She was the reason for his suffering.

She Was The Reason His Wife Died.

AND, SHE WAS THE REASON FOR HIS BABY DYING!

Out of the two hundred employees that worked the warehouse floor, every last one of them gave the exact same account of what was heard from one end of the building to the other, before her tormentor launched into an all-out attack on Lucia.

I'M GOING TO KILL YOU!

And she would have died in his strangling hands if it had not been for her fellow workers, and the best friend any girl could have, tearing him away from her crumpled body.

Instead of dying with Mr. Blackwell's hands around her throat, Lucia passed away in the arms of Lavinia Codona.

The only person who had any inkling of why this had just happened.

She was also the only other girl who was suffering from Blackwell's unwanted advances too.

And like all good Gypsy's, a righteous curse is never bragged about to strangers and those who are not of the traveling clans.

That's why, if you just happen to be one of the lucky ones, this story is only told around those darkened nights when someone is wanting to know about Lucia and the outcome of her actions.

Is there still power in her curse?

And the questionable answer is always the same.

Do you see a Blackwell's baby blanket anywhere in the vicinity?

Do you?

You will never see such a thing in our camps or anywhere near a Gypsy.

Normal, everyday people are an entirely different ball game.

They love his Baby Blankets.

I'm willing to bet that you might have had one yourself.

Even to this day, Doctors are still unsure what causes SIDS in a baby. They have many theories, but no answers to that unsolved question.

But Gypsy's know.

They have always known.

If someone's baby unexpectedly passes away with a baby blanket in the crib, and it's a Blackwell's creation, the curse of Lucia has most likely struck once again.

If your young and always sickly, is there a blanket from Blackwell's in the room?

And, if others get sick and pass away around the same time as the baby did; were they wrapped in a Blackwell's blanket as they mourned.

If so, you really should check your own blanket.

Because, if it's from Blackwell's, Lucia's curse is coming for you.

As unto the Blackwell's, so unto the buyer.

Let the curse of a Slow, Painful, and Wasting Death befall the baby and all those who purchase this and all other blankets.

254

QUOTES FROM THE GREENMAN.

Now some people sleep with their windows wide opened,

While others keep them tightly closed.

But, bugs can still get in.

That's because they come in all shapes, styles, and sizes.

So, no matter what you do,

They're still going to get in and eat you.

Well, it's nighty-night time.

And as The Greenman always says to those who are ready to be tucked in,

Good night.

Sleep tight.

Because the bedbugs,

Will always bite.

256

SCARAB GARRAB.

Beetles can be fun

And beetles can be stinky

But if you see a Scarab

Run away quickly.

These little beetles

Don't just spray and bite

They're a one-way ticket

To the afterlife.

The little dung beetle

Knows the day is short

It must lay its eggs

Inside a cohort.

Too bad there's not a body

Laying just around

Oh, look, here's one now

Upon you he has found.

Now you can turn about

And out sprint him fast

But once a Scarab sees you

Your soul he's set to task.

Now onward to

What must be

Answer his questions

To satisfy he.

To escape a horrid fate

For his eggs not incubate

These three questions you must know

Or in your gullet they all go.

Now onward to

What must be

Answer this question

To satisfy he.

And choose your answer well

Or in your gullet

Garrab's eggs will dwell.

When we came to be

Was Khepri the God you see

Or amongst the brothers

Were there chosen others.

Choose your answer well

Or in your gullet

Garrab's eggs will dwell.

Now onward to

What must be

Answer this question

To satisfy He.

The Middle Kingdom

Egypt saw

Did I rub

Their necks so raw?

Try not to hem and haw

Or, you will lose it all.

Choose your answer well

Or in your gullet

Garrab's eggs will dwell.

Now onward to

What must be

Answer this question

To satisfy he.

When the New Kingdom finally dawned

Did we sleep where Pharos fawned?

Hurry up

And answer quick

Or Scarab's knife

Will lickety-slip.

Choose your answer well

Or in your gullet

Garrab's eggs will dwell.

Now onward to

What must be

If you were lucky

And answered all three.

Is the sun still risen

Or gone away

This next answer

Decides your day.

Choose your answer well

Or in your gullet

Garrab's eggs will dwell.

Now onward to

What must be

Answer that question

To satisfy he.

For if the sun did sat

And you didn't win

Into Hades

Your spirit grims

Full of eggs

Garrab's batch

And once they've fed

They'll meatily hatch.

Now onward to

What must be

Garrab isn't

Done with thee.

There's one more thing

He needs to do

Before the last

Of you is through.

To be a Scarab

Of utmost high

It's now time

Your soul must die.

So in the morning

He can rise

To pick another

For egg mother.

Now onward to

Who must be

Answer these questions

To satisfy he.

Choose your answer well

Or in your gullet

Garrab's eggs will dwell.

268

QUOTES FROM THE GREENMAN.

If people could say one thing about you after your gone,

Let it be this.

Every minute that life offered,

You lived it to its brightest and fullest.

You waisted not one drop of that precious gift on nonsense, self-hatred, nor the tearing down, humiliation, or destruction of others.

You lived In Peace and Harmony with any and everyone.

Out of love, you chose Ascension instead of Descension.

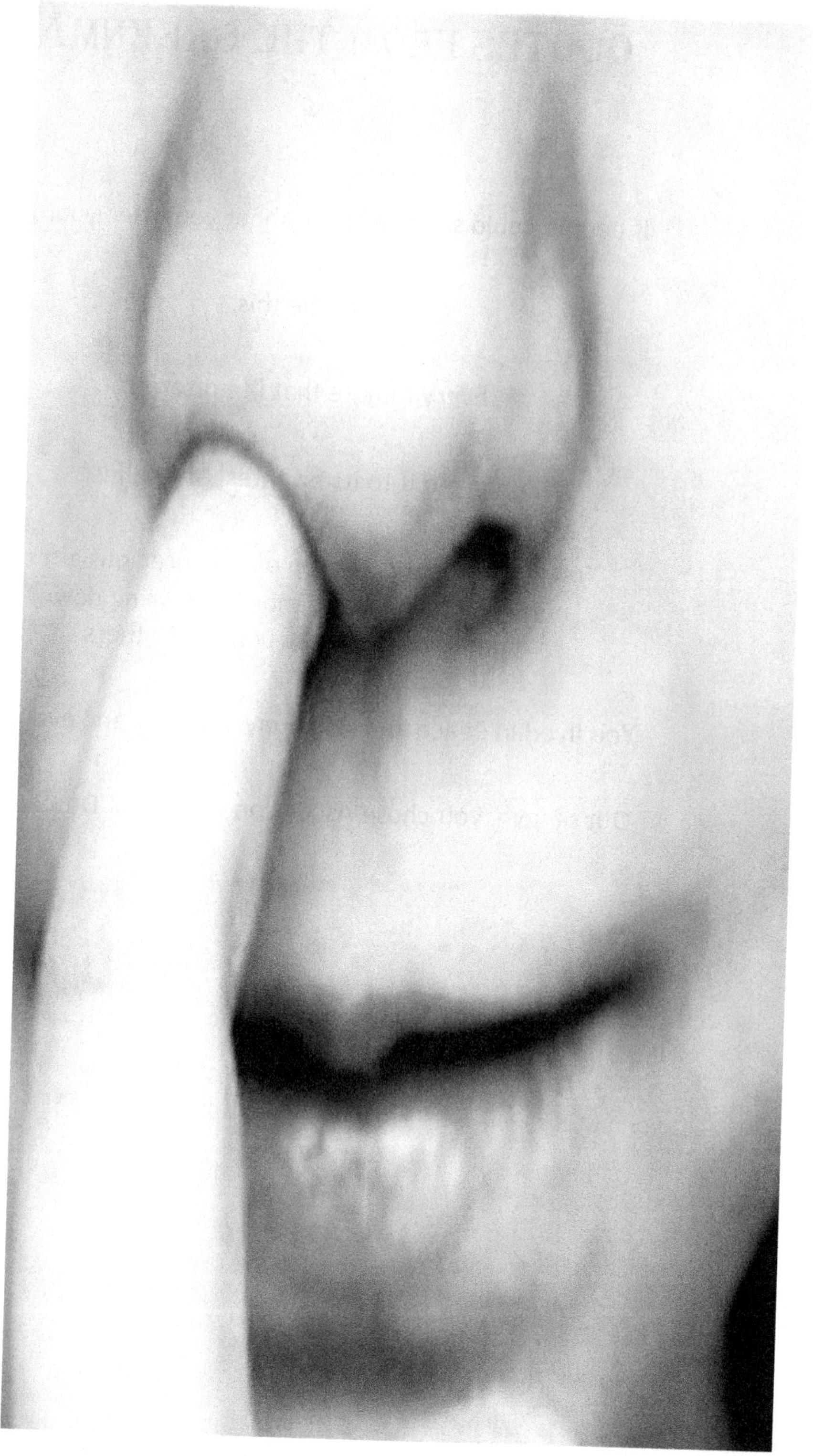

EWWGARI BOOGARI.

Did you know

The quickest way

To losing all your friends.

Snotty bubbles

Boogery whoas

And always a finger

Up your nose.

Ewwgari Boogari

Kills that which it touches

Even a King

His Queen

And their Duchess.

Now we all know

This plague is vast

With no escapes

From its deadly blast.

Ewwgari Boogari

Kills that which it touches

Even a King

His Queen

And their Duchess.

A game of marbles

Can end real quick

When the slimy glass

Starts to stick.

That is why

You should never pick

Or all your friends

Will end up sick.

Ewwgari Boogari

Kills that which it touches

Even a King

His Queen

And their Duchess.

Now as your nose turns bright red

And the snot begins to thicken

Everyone knows your deadly now

Upon your plague they'll sicken.

Ewwgari Boogari

Kills that which it touches

Even a King

His Queen

And their Duchess

Now there's a way

To spread him quick

And make your friends

Extremely sick.

Cough over there

Over here too

On all cleaned surfaces

You must Boogari spew.

Ewwgari Boogari

Kills that which it touches

Even a King

His Queen

And their Duchess

As the petri dish

You carry inside

Multiplies and Sickens

All from you

We should run

Lickety split and quicken.

Ewwgari Boogari

Kills that which it touches

Even a King

His Queen

And their Duchess.

With boogers green

Chewy brown Ew

Sickly yellow and very runny white too

It's definitely time

To step back from you.

Stop picking your nose

Like we're not here

With fingers deep for that treat

That you'll sniff, lick, and most definitely eat.

Ewwgari Boogari

Kills that which it touches

Even a King

His Queen

And their Duchess.

I share all this

In hopes to live

And for your benefit.

Stop picking your nose.

Eating your boogers.

And running your friends away.

For if you wish

For them to stay

Booger

Picking

Ends

Today.

Ewwgari Boogari

Kills that which it touches

Even a king

His Queen

And their Duchess.

280

QUOTES FROM THE GREENMAN.

Did you know that parents are afraid of monsters too?

For some reason, the little critters are always

Drawn to their bedroom when Mom and Dad are noisy.

That's why the parents of little monsters send

Winkin, Blinkin, and Nod to their room.

They know just what to do with little kids who refuse to

Sleep in their own beds.

And here they come now!

282

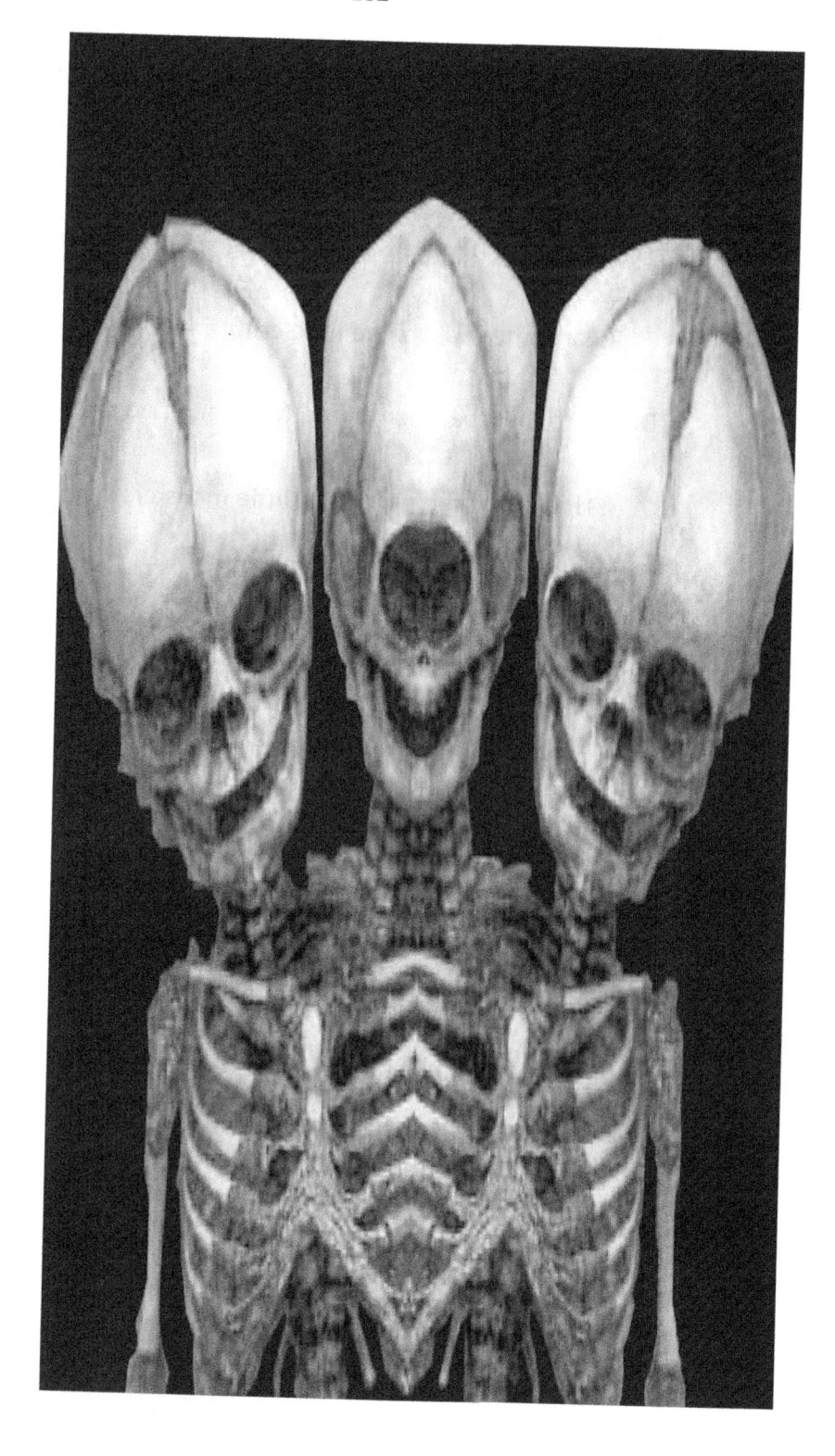

WINKIN, BLINKIN, AND NOD.

Did you know

That there's a monster

For those who stay awake?

He has two arms

And both legs too

But above the shoulder

Sits more than a few

And all three heads

Will come for you.

Winkin

Blinkin

And Nod

Know just what to do

If you refuse to bed

After your parents said.

There are things

That they need

And non-sleeping kids

Will fear their dread

As they give up

Their sweet little heads.

Winkin wants your eye lids

While Blinkin takes an eye

And Nod needs your neck

So, tonight you're the pie.

A slice of you they'll take

A piece here and there

But if you'd been asleep

All your parts you'd have keeped.

They hide in the corner or under your bed

Waiting to see if you did

Exactly as

Your Parents said.

Will you lay down

Your sleepy head

Or, stay wide awake

And play instead.

Winkin

Blinkin

And Nod

Know just what to do

If you refuse to bed

After your parents said.

Winkin wants your eye lids

While Blinkin takes an eye

And Nod needs your neck

So, tonight you're the pie.

A slice of you they'll take

A piece here and there

But if you'd been asleep

All your parts you'd have keeped.

Now as you nimbly play

Quieter than a mouse

They'll begin to move

And creep around the house.

Tiptoeing around

Touching things not

Leaving no clue

Of what happened to you.

And when you are found

That very next day

Your horrified parents

Will have but one thing to say.

The last time I saw them

Was right before bed

I told them to sleep

Or I'd off their little head.

I didn't mean

The threat that I said

That's why I left it

To the monster instead.

I told them that the brothers three

Will come get them

If they refuse to sleep

And then shared the story

Of they who creep.

Did you know

That there's a monster

For those who stay awake?

He has two arms

And both legs too

But above the shoulder

Sits more than a few.

Three deformed heads

That are coming for you.

Winkin

Blinkin

And Nod

Know just what to do

If you refuse to bed

After your parents said.

There are things

That they need

And non-sleeping kids

Will fear their dread

As they give up

Their sweet little heads.

Winkin wants your eye lids

While Blinkin takes an eye

And Nod needs your neck

So tonight you're the pie

A slice of you they'll take

A piece here and there

But if you'd been asleep

All your parts you'd have keeped.

They hide in the corner or under your bed

Waiting to see if you did

Exactly as

Mommy said.

Will you lay down

Your sleepy head

Or stay wide awake

And play instead.

So when it comes to beddy-bye time

Are you going to stay awake or do as you're told.

Remember this before you do

A Three Headed Monster

Is hungering for you.

And if you refuse to follow through

After Daddy had to say it too

Winkin

Blinkin

And Nod

Know just what to do.

Winkin wants your eye lids

While Blinkin takes an eye

And Nod needs your neck

So tonight you're the pie.

A slice of you they'll take

A piece here and there

But if you'd been asleep

All your parts you'd have keeped.

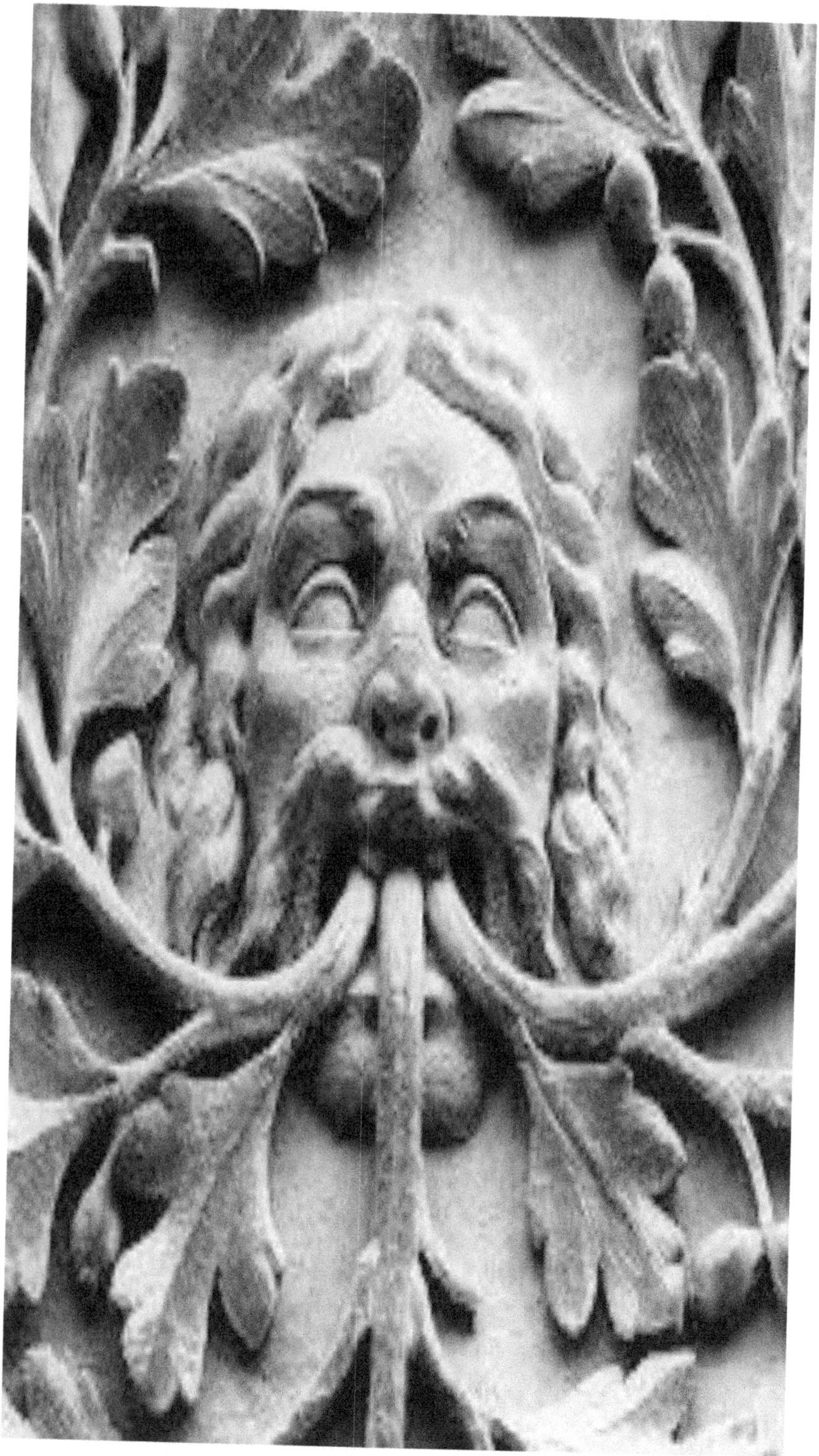

QUOTES FROM THE GREENMAN.

As you read this last page, please remember this.

YOU are Unique.

YOU are Fragile.

And YOU are Much Stronger than you think.

YOUR Feelings Do Matter.

And so does Your Opinions.

Everything about YOU has Value.

And YOU are worth MORE THAN GOLD.

And So Is That Person standing next to You.

If You wish to be greater than You ever could be,

RESPECT The People who also walk this planet with You.

WHETHER THEY DESERVE IT OR NOT!

BECAUSE, WE OURSELVES, DON'T ALWAYS DESERVE IT AFTER SOME OF THE HORRIBLE THINGS WE HAVE WILLINGLY SAID AND DONE TO THOSE WHO SHOULD

NEVER HAVE RECIEVED THE BRUNT OF OUR SHAMELESS AND IMMORAL ACTIONS.

Man, Woman, Children, The Poor, Homeless, Downtrodden, Geek, Nerd, Sexually Different, Outcast, Believer in a God or not, and Every Other SOUL which lives, breathes and walks this planet with You and I.

WE ALL BELONG HERE JUST AS MUCH AS EVERYONE ELSE.

Honor Their Value and I Promise Most Will Honor Yours.

If not, Our World Will Never Heal.

It's time for ALL OF US to Cast Away Hate, Judgment, and Persecution

THE TIME FOR UNCONDITIONAL LOVE IS NOW NEEDED MORE THAN EVER.

IT'S TIME TO TRANSCEND.

Sincerely, The Greenman.

A touch of INSANITY Is Required for good writing.